A curse lays heavy upon the land.
Summer's eves taste
the lonely chill of winter.
The once-emerald hills now lie
fallow and barren.
Hunger gnaws at man and beast.

Five must journey north,
seeking an end to the spell.
Yet only one can cross the final river
whose opposite shore holds a paradise,
green and fruitful.
But will Myrddin allow this seeker
to fulfill his quest?

Also published by HarperPrism

*Roar*

# ROAR

## THE CAULDRON

A novel by

☙ SEAN KIERNAN ☙

based on the Universal Television series
created by Shaun Cassidy and Ron Koslow

HarperPrism
*A Division of HarperCollins Publishers*

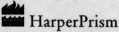 HarperPrism

*A Division of* HarperCollins*Publishers*
10 East 53rd Street, New York, NY 10022-5299

This is a work of fiction. The characters, incidents, and dialogues are products of the author's imagination and are not to be construed as real. Any resemblance to actual events or persons, living or dead, is entirely coincidental.

ISBN 0-06-105936-6

HarperCollins®, 📕®, and HarperPrism®
are trademarks of HarperCollins Publishers, Inc.

Cover photograph © 1997 by Tim Bauer/Universal Television

First printing: June 1998

Printed in the United States of America

Visit HarperPrism on the World Wide Web at
http://www.harperprism.com

❖ 10 9 8 7 6 5 4 3 2 1

You don't win the favor of the ancient gods by being good, but by being *bold*.

—Anita Brookner

# ROAR

## THE CAULDRON

# ONE

## THE HOUND OF CULANN

—1—

The day was chill, the sounds of the sea lost and mournful beyond the fog-cloaked moors that ran south toward the cliffs. Conor raised his head and sniffed the damp air.

"Smells like rain."

Fergus, riding a huge roan stallion, pulled his cloak tighter about his shoulders and grunted. "What do you expect? It's winter."

Catlin, riding behind with Tully, sniffed loudly. Tully grinned at her. "Say something," he said.

"You jusd wand do hear me talk like dis. I cand helb it. It's by dose."

Tully laughed, but when he saw the miserable expression on her face, he sobered. "It's not getting any better?"

She shook her head. "Gedding worse."

Fergus snorted. "Of course it is, lad. We're

dragging the poor girl all over this forsaken wilderness, when she needs rest, a warm fire, and . . . and chicken soup!"

Conor stared at him. "Chicken soup?"

Fergus reddened. "I can make chicken soup."

Tully said, "Sure. But first you have to find a chicken." He waved at the bleak gray landscape that stretched out on all sides. "No chickens here. Barely any grass. Maybe you could make grass soup."

Conor tugged on the reins of his own gray mare and brought her to a halt. "Look," he said. "I'm sorry. I know it's hard. But we've got to find that magician. You said it yourself, Tully. There's a curse on the Land. And with Galen and Blas gone, there's nobody to help us. Unless you've changed your mind about your own powers."

Tully shook his head. "Galen taught me a lot, but nothing like that. I can feel the curse. It's strong, Conor. It's eating away at the Land, at the Alliance, at everything. You're right, we need a real sorcerer, but . . ." He trailed off and stared around, his expression dismal. "All we know about this Myrddin are just rumors. He may not even exist."

"You said you felt something yesterday."

"Something, yes . . . but what, I don't really know."

Fergus snorted again, louder, his mustache quivering. "Most likely your empty belly griping at you, boy. That's what you felt."

Conor sighed as he leaned back in his saddle. "Well, Fergus, what would you have me do? Give up? Go back and watch everything fall apart? You know what's happening. This winter has been the hardest even the Old Women remember. The fields are dying. Sheep going to the wolves. And Diana pecking away at the Alliance, a warrior here, a family there, even a small clan or two. If it keeps on like this, we could lose everything. Everything all of us have worked for. Is that what you want?"

Fergus looked away. "I still say . . ." He spat suddenly. "Magicians. Pah. Maybe we'd do better to talk to those warriors who've decided they like the Roman strumpet so well. That seems like a better idea than wandering around in this damned wilderness without so much as a sniff of your sorcerer."

"Diana was wiser than I gave her credit for. She stored the largest part of her harvests, and now she has food to offer as bribes. I should have paid attention. But I didn't—and now it's too late."

"Dode be so hard on yourself, Codor," Catlin said. "How could you hab known?"

"I should have known! Isn't that what a leader is supposed to do? Know things? Especially when it's the welfare of his people at stake?" Suddenly his shoulders slumped. "Or maybe it's just that I'm not much of a leader . . ."

Tully rammed his heels into the ribs of his mount and came abreast of Conor. "Don't talk like that. I told you, it's magic! There *is* a curse, no matter what this old bag of farts says. And you're not going to fix it by talking." He turned and glared at Fergus, whose mustache was quivering even more strongly.

"Bag of farts am I, you little swamp rat? Maybe

I'll stick *you* into a bag . . ." He raised one brawny arm.

"Hold on!" Conor said. "Look at us. Fighting like children." He leaned over and slapped Fergus on the back. "Calm down, you old goat. It's this damned weather. It's got us all on edge. But we won't solve anything by brawling among ourselves."

This time Fergus's snort sounded more like the crack of a whip, but he lowered his arm. "Well, you may be right. For once."

"Look. We're all cold and tired, and Catlin's sick. As soon as we find a likely spot, we'll lie up and make camp. Someplace out of the wind. Get some rest, get some food in our bellies, and we'll all feel better."

Fergus made a grumbling noise deep in his chest, but after a moment he nodded. "Up ahead there, that rise. It looks like there's trees, maybe even a spring."

Conor looked over his shoulder at Catlin. "Hang on, Cat. We'll have you all nice and bundled up in a jiffy."

She sneezed. They set off again. Nobody mentioned the saddle packs on their horses, which had been growing thinner for the past two weeks.

No chicken soup tonight. Maybe stone soup . . .

—2—

The land rippled slowly up toward the low hills, growing stonier as they proceeded. To the west the pale white disk of the sun sank lower, becoming a diffuse streak of light. A wind sprang up out of the north, harsh and biting, and bearing a whiff of some foul odor.

Fergus wrinkled his nose. "Nasty . . ."

Conor glanced at him. "It smells like . . . something familiar."

Fergus regarded him sourly. "Have you forgotten already, boy? That's the stink you get when you piss on a fire. Wet, burned wood. You smelled it in the ruins of your father's keep."

Conor winced, and looked away. They rode on, each wrapped in cloaks and silence. Distances here were deceptive. Though the chain of low hills looked close enough, it took them another hour to reach the hem of the sparse woods that clung to the rocky slopes. The remnants of a path ran along the edge of the trees, and they guided their horses onto it.

Fergus loosened his sword in the scabbard that rode across his back. "A path," he said. "Doesn't look like anybody's used it in a while."

Conor eyed the faint dirt trail. "Somebody must have used it once." He looked up at the trees, now shading from dusty green to gray as dusk bleached the colors out of the world. "No stream up there."

Fergus shook his head. "Maybe that way?"

Conor nodded, and urged his mount toward the left. The others fell in behind. A few moments later they heard a sudden flapping, like a blanket whipping in the wind. A huge blackbird exploded from the top of the woods, climbed straight up, then dived at them, beak so wide they could see the bright orange of its gullet.

"Awwkk! Awwkk!"

It flew so close above their heads that Fergus raised one arm to shield himself. A moment later the bird arrowed out across the moor and vanished in the gathering gloom.

Fergus and Conor glanced at each other. "An omen?" Fergus muttered.

"No, a damned bird," Tully answered. "Let's go. I'm freezing my butt off."

—3—

The light was nearly gone, the sky overhead a dull, leaden gray, when they crested a small ridge and saw the homestead below.

Conor raised one hand and pulled his mare to a halt. Fergus pressed close, his palm above his eyes, squinting. "What is that? A farm?"

"It looks like some kind of smithy. See, there's still smoke rising from the forge."

Fergus shook his head. "I can't see that far. This light is so bad . . ."

Tully snorted. "You mean you're going blind in your old age."

"I can see well enough to slap you off that horse, smart mouth," Fergus rumbled.

Conor ignored them. There was something about the stedding—two log buildings thatched with moldy straw, a stone corral, an unroofed forge, a dusty courtyard—forlorn, yet he felt an air of menace about it. As if it were long deserted, yet still inhabited by . . . something.

"We could make camp here," he said, gesturing at the ground on the side of the path.

Tully came forward, his eyes sharp and bright. "No, see by the forge? That's a well. There's water down there." He pointed at the stony ground on either side of the path, then at the dark, twisted oaks looming beyond. "No water up here. Nothing for Fergus's damned chicken soup."

Conor looked at Fergus and raised his eyebrows. Fergus shrugged. "Tully's right. We should go down. If they'll let us camp in the courtyard, all to the good. And if it's empty, we could borrow it for the night. Sleep under a roof."

"The place looks empty," Conor said.

"There's a fire."

"A damned stinking one," Tully added. Then, with sudden decision, he leaned forward and said, "Nothing tried, nothing gotten," and booted his horse again. A moment later he was twenty paces ahead, crouched low over his saddle, galloping for the stedding.

His thin cry floated back toward them. "Hallooo, the house! Hallooo!"

"Crazy brat," Fergus growled. "Get his fool head knocked off."

"Wait!"

But Fergus was already hot on Tully's trail. "Idiots," Conor muttered, glancing back at Catlin. She wiped her nose on the back of her sleeve. "Well, are you goig to just sid there?"

Conor sighed, slapped his mare, and the two of them pounded after.

—— 4 ——

"The water's good, anyway," Fergus said.

They were gathered around the broken stone ring of the well, watching Tully climb like a monkey up the slick, slime-covered stones, a dripping water bag slung over his shoulder. As his hand came over the edge, Fergus grabbed his wrist and yanked him the rest of the way, like pulling a cork from a bottle.

"Whoa, watch it! You almost broke my arm!" But Tully was grinning. "Now you can make chicken soup."

Fergus glowered at the courtyard. "Really? Now we've got water, but do you see any chickens?"

Catlin had wandered away toward the forge, an ancient stone firepit heaped with shapeless, smoldering lengths. Conor was wiping down his mare with his extra shirt when he heard her call. Something in her voice brought his head up sharply, a frown creasing his forehead.

"Codor, over here!"

He stepped around his horse and saw her bending over the firepit. "What? What's wrong?"

"Come *here!*"

As he moved toward her, he slid his sword from its scabbard, as much a reflex as anything. She sounded frightened. It took a lot to frighten Catlin. He was vaguely aware of Fergus and Tully coming up behind, the sound of their metal a steely whisper in his ears.

"What?"

She was still leaning forward. The wind had

shifted, and was blowing the worst of the stench away from them, but the smell was still overpowering: charred, wet, rotten.

"Here," she said. "Just look."

"I don't see . . ." Then his eyes widened. "Are those—"

"Bodes," she said. "Human bodes."

Tully made a gagging sound. The firepit was about as wide as a man was tall, and heaped high with bones. A dull red glow smoldered in the heart of the grisly pile.

"By the Dark Ones," Fergus breathed, stepping forward. He poked at the edge with the tip of his sword. A charred skull fell out of the pit to the muddy earth, eyeholes blank and staring. Part of the skull was cracked away, as if something had dealt it a tremendous blow.

They stared at it.

"I dod wad to stay here," Catlin said. She sniffed the stink of burning skin. "I cad smell id, and I cand smell anythig."

At her mention of the word *skin,* Conor realized what those crispy little bits attached to the smoldering bones were. His stomach gave a greasy heave.

"What's that?" Tully said. Conor wheeled around, his sword up and questing.

"Where?"

Tully held a knife in his right hand, eight inches of razor-edged steel gleaming against the last of the light. Now, like a magic trick, a knife was in his other hand too. "Did you hear it? *There . . .*"

They all heard it then. A slow, ragged exhalation, like a hide bellows with a hole in it. Deep, bubbling, harsh. And a sudden cascade of horny clicks. Big claws, maybe, scrabbling on stone, seeking purchase.

Coming from behind the main house. Louder . . .

It exploded around the corner of the house, big as a horse, ropes of drool trailing from its yellowed fangs, its tail stiff and ears standing straight up. It crossed half the courtyard in one single bound, and now they could see its eyes, great red pools of fire. A dog, but like no dog he'd ever seen. A hellhound.

Then it was among them, a whirlwind, snapping, barking, slashing, legs like small tree trunks, claws as sharp as daggers. Conor felt a stunning blow and something gave way inside his chest. A rib, probably. He picked himself up, groaning, each breath like an arrow in his side. He was a good ten feet away from the monster, who had Fergus and Catlin backed up against the firepit. Tully lay a few paces away, crumpled and unmoving. Even from this distance, Conor could see the hilt of one of Tully's knives protruding from the left eye of the snarling beast.

Trying to hold his rib in place with one hand, he raised his sword and dashed back into the fray. The monstrous hound stood nearly as tall at the shoulder as Fergus, who was holding it off— barely—with great sweeps of his broadsword. Catlin crouched behind the old warrior, desperately trying to string her bow, her face a pale blob of terror.

Conor hacked at the back leg of the thing, a

wild, off-balance swing aimed at the hamstring. He felt the edge of his blade chunk solidly into bone, saw blood gout into the thick, matted fur. But instead of crippling the beast, he only enraged it further. It swung around with shocking speed, jaws wide, howling in pain and rage. A wash of hot, fetid breath belched into Conor's face, rank with the stink of carrion.

He leaned backwards, but the sudden movement sent a stab of agony roaring up from his ribs, doubling him over. He tripped, fell backwards, and the hound was on him.

Claws raked his shoulders. Saliva, burning hot, dripped on his face, as the dog's huge maw yawned wide. Conor reached up, grabbed the knife hilt protruding from the ruined eye, and twisted.

The bellow that followed nearly broke his eardrums, but the dreadful specter retreated. Conor rolled to the side and scrambled to his feet, just in time to see a long arrow-shaft sprout from the dog's neck.

Dimly he heard Catlin shouting in triumph as she nocked another arrow and let fly. Grimly Conor raised his sword and waded in, hacking and slashing at the beast's dripping muzzle.

Off to his left he saw a small, dark figure rushing through the murk. A moment later Tully, a long, bleeding gash across his face, landed on the hound's neck, his remaining knife rising and falling.

"No!" Conor shouted, but it was too late. With a single vicious shake, the hell-dog pitched Tully into the air, and swiped at him as he fell. Tully screamed once, then lay silent.

"Tully!" Conor moved toward him, but the hound barred the way, as deadly as ever, though now dripping red from a dozen wounds as it crouched over Tully's prone form.

Fergus, roaring his own battle cry, moved in again at the rear of the dog, trying for its hamstring. He had better luck than Conor, because the animal suddenly screamed as its left hind leg gave way. It sat down hard, crushing Tully, then dragged itself around to face the new threat.

Though wounded, it was still faster than anything Conor had ever seen. Fergus was too close to escape the battering ram of the hound's huge skull. Conor heard a sickening crunch, and saw Fergus go flying through the air. He landed on the smoldering firepit, screamed, and rolled off.

Now the hound was facing Catlin. Cool as ice, she drew her bow again and planted an arrow directly between its gaping jaws. The beast crunched down on the shaft like a toothpick and lurched toward her, forcing her back.

Conor grabbed Tully's shoulder and dragged the fallen boy several paces away from the struggle, then turned back, gasping from the pain in his side.

Catlin had retreated around the firepit and was fitting another arrow to her bowstring. But in the murk she didn't see she'd wedged herself into a corner from which there was no escape. The hound did, though: It was bunching its good hind leg for a leap across the pit. Conor did the calculation almost instantly. His sword was too puny, and there was no time.

He rushed to the left, the side where the beast was blinded. Some of the charred bones in the pit were huge, broken off with jagged, spiny tips. He grabbed one of these, nearly as tall as he was, and kept on going.

The beast didn't see him as its great muscles contracted, then exploded as it hurled itself across the smoking pile. But it was injured, and not quite as fast as it had been before. Conor arrived first, planted the butt of the great bone in the mud, and braced it as well as he could, an instant before the hound landed belly-first on it, its own great weight immediately forcing it down harder.

Conor leaped away as the thing impaled itself. It bellowed in agony. Blood gushed out, splattering both Conor and Catlin. It seared like boiling water as it splashed over them, and they both retreated, trying to wipe the burning stuff off their skin as the monster hound raged further into its death throes.

It thrashed, heaved itself against the firepit, scattering bones in every direction, then lurched back the other way. But it was dying. Its ear-splitting cries gradually lessened until, with one final, piteous groan, it collapsed entirely and lay still.

Silence.

"By the gods . . ." Conor breathed, leaning against Catlin for support.

From the other side of what remained of the pit, Fergus staggered up. "Are you all right?" he shouted.

"We're okay," Conor replied. He felt Catlin move away from him.

"Tully!" she cried.

—5—

Darkness had fallen hard, the stars and moon obscured now by a drifting, malevolent mist. The stench of the hound's corpse, cooking slowly on the remains of the firepit, made their eyes water and burned their nostrils.

They were huddled around a tiny fire Fergus had built. The old warrior was busy wrapping torn strips of his cloak tightly around Conor's ribs, as Conor sat naked from the waist up and shivering. Fergus said, "Hold your breath, now," and made a final yank on the makeshift bandage, then tied it off.

"You're going to be sore, but I think it will hold all right. That rib is cracked, not broken, is my guess."

Conor nodded. He did feel better with the binding holding his bones steady. He turned gingerly and looked at where Catlin was crouched over Tully.

"Cat? How is he?"

"Not good. There's a bad cut on his belly, and something's wrong with his head. A big lump, and blood in his ears."

"Huh. Means his skull's probably cracked," Fergus said dourly. He glanced at Conor, started to say something, then thought better of it. But Conor caught the movement and sighed.

"I know," he said. "It's my fault."

"Conor . . ." Catlin said.

"No, it is. I brought us here. Fergus didn't want to come."

"Now, boy," Fergus said gently. "I didn't mean . . ." He stopped. "True, I was against it, but even I didn't think of anything like this."

Conor shook his head. "What *was* it, Fergus? A hound that big? I've never seen anything like it. Or heard of it."

"Of course you have. Or have you forgotten all the songs about the High Ones? Blas would know right away. And so would you, if you think about it."

"No, I . . ."

"Look around. What is this place?"

"A smithy . . ."

"Exactly. Probably one of the first songs you ever heard the bards sing." Then, nodding to himself, Fergus began to sing in a slow, deep baritone.

*King Conor went to Culann*
*The best swordsmith in the Land*
*With Conor's nephew Setanta*
*And the boys of the warrior band . . .*

He stopped, and looked up. "You remember how it went, don't you?"

Conor's eyes were wide. "Culann's smithy was guarded by a great hellhound. Setanta accidentally entered the smithy when the hound was loose, and it attacked him. With teeth like an armory and eyes like red-hot coals. Setanta killed it with his bare hands, and then promised Culann he would take its place. And he changed his name to Cu Chulann, the Hound of Culann. Cuchulann," he whispered softly. "The greatest hero our Land has ever known."

"Aye," Fergus muttered. He turned his head and spat. "And you killed this hound, Conor."

Conor stared at him in silence for a long moment. "You don't think . . ."

"I don't know *what* I think. Except I feel magic all around me. It makes my skin itch, and I don't like it."

Conor went silent again, but Catlin was having none of it. She left Tully and joined them. "I don't care about all that! Tully's hurt. We have to find somebody to help him."

Fergus eyed her from beneath his shelf of a brow. "And who do you suggest, lass? None of us are healers. And I don't see any sorcerers or root women coming out of this wilderness, either." He spat again, this time into the fire. "Also, in case you've forgotten, our horses and all our supplies are gone."

Conor winced. It was true. The attack of the hound had terrified their animals, who'd fled with everything they had except the clothes on their backs. Maybe the horses would return, but Conor was dubious. Horses were sensitive to smells, and the carrion reek that polluted the air hereabouts would probably keep them running until they were beyond returning.

Fergus seemed to sense his thoughts. "They're likely headed south by now. Heading for home. Like we should be."

Conor sighed. Fergus's words had the bitter bite of truth. Yet to return meant failure, and maybe even the destruction of the Alliance.

This was the part of being a leader that he

hated the most. Glorious fights, thrilling triumphs, even at the risk of death—those were one thing. But the hard, hopeless decisions, made in the bowels of the night . . .

Tully. The Alliance. He raised his head, wincing as the movement tugged at his bad rib. "Tomorrow we can make a travois. Something to carry Tully on. Fergus, you and Catlin are in better shape than I am. You can drag him. So you head back south, and try to get to the Druids in time to help him."

Catlin saw it coming. "Conor, you can't . . ."

"And I'll continue on north." He stared at the girl. "Cat, I *have* to. I have to find this magician, this Myrddin. I *can't* let the Alliance just fall apart." He paused, glanced over at Tully's silent shape. "It's what Tully would want, I think," he said softly. "He might die, you know, no matter what we do. And if he does, I will not let his life go in vain. I just won't."

Catlin glanced back and forth uncertainly between the two men. Conor's face was pale but determined. Fergus's blocky features were set as stones.

"Maybe . . ." she said. "If we find this magician, he could help Tully?"

Fergus growled.

"No, think about it," she went on. "Conor is sure he's around here somewhere. Even Tully said he sensed a magical presence. And it's a journey of weeks to get back south." She shook her head. "He's bad, Fergus. I don't think he'd survive the trip. If we're going to help him, it's going to have to be soon."

Fergus said, "Aye, and you remember the barren lands we've already come through. We've been living out of our packs for days now. Without supplies, we might not even make it ourselves." He sighed heavily. "I don't like this at all, Conor, but the girl's probably right. We have to go on now. We have no choice."

He glared across the fire. "Damn you, we have no choice!"

Conor nodded. "I'm sorry."

"Hound of Culann," Fergus muttered. Suddenly he stood up and walked away from the fire, vanishing into the gloom that surrounded him.

"It's all my fault," Conor said a second time.

Catlin moved around the fire, knelt before him, and touched his cheek. "I don't think it's a matter of fault, Conor," she said softly. He realized she was shivering, and he felt a thrill jangle through his own bones at her next words.

"I think it's a matter of fate . . ."

# ƆWO

## ƆHE RIVER OF AVALLON

—1—

Conor woke to a cold, dreary morning. He opened his eyes and stared up at a sky the color of an old cook-pot, lumpy and mottled.

For a moment he wasn't quite sure where he was. Then it all came back. Without thinking, he moved to get his elbows under him and sit up, but as soon as he tried, he let out a low, involuntary groan. The muscles along his ribs had tightened up as he slept, and now it felt as if somebody was grinding the edge of a saw blade along the bones there.

"Stings a bit, eh, lad?" Fergus called cheerfully from the other side of the fire.

Conor managed to make it to a sitting position. "What are you so damned happy about?"

"Things could be worse," Fergus said. "Catlin was awake early, and the girl still has her eye. As

this rabbit discovered when it poked its nose out."
He gestured toward the fire.

Conor saw that Fergus had found a battered
iron pot somewhere. It rested in the center of the
glowing coals, bubbling merrily, full of rich broth
and chunks of rabbit meat. Conor's nose twitched.

"That smells great." Suddenly he realized he
was starving.

"Better than that blasted hound," Fergus
agreed. He leaned forward and stirred the pot carefully. "Could do with some greens or something,
but it's about ready."

"Where's Cat?"

"She went off looking for things we could use
for a travois. This place is pretty well empty. Nothing
in the buildings but dust and broken furniture."

Conor nodded, thinking about it—and not lik-
ing the direction his thoughts were taking. "But
the firepit was still hot. And those bones . . ."

"Aye," Fergus said somberly. "It doesn't make
any sense. But there it is." His broad shoulders
twitched. "I have to confess, I'll be glad when we've
got this place to the back of us. One way or the
other." Fergus grinned at him. "So, how's the ribs
this morning?"

Conor moved gingerly. "Ouch. Still stiff. But I
think they'll loosen up."

"Yes, cracked ribs. They won't kill you. They'll
just make you wish you were dead."

"The thought seems to give you a fair amount
of pleasure, you old boar."

Fergus chuckled. "Just glad it's you and not
me, lad."

"Hmph."

"Conor! You're awake." Catlin came around the corner of the largest house, hauling two long stakes of rough-hewn lumber. "Roof poles," she said. "I think they'll do for the travois." She glanced at the fire. "Mmm. That looks good, Fergus."

"Well, it's not chicken soup." His eyebrows rose. "You sound better, girl."

"I feel better. My nose cleared up, at least—and I can smell your soup. Is it ready?"

They ate with makeshift spoons carved out of bits of wood scattered about, Fergus slurping noisily and congratulating himself on his cooking skills.

"Save some of the broth," Catlin said. "When it's cool I'll try to get a little into Tully."

Fergus craned his neck and eyed the unconscious boy dubiously. "Be careful not to choke him."

"I will." She sighed. "I hope his cuts don't start to rot."

Fergus shrugged. "In the hands of the High Ones now, lass."

"No, in our hands too!" Conor broke in. "If we can find this magician, surely he can help. That's what magicians do."

"If they feel like it," Fergus said. "Longinus was a magician too. I just hope this one, if we find him, is more like Galen or Blas than that damned Roman sorcerer."

He grunted, slapped his knees, and stood. "I'll cut up one of the cloaks for the travois." The sky had lightened somewhat, but even though the wind had dissipated most of the heavy ground mist, it still carried a harsh edge. "And we'll need another to cover him, keep him warm."

"Take my cloak," Conor said instantly.

Fergus nodded. "I'll use mine, as well."

"Hey, wait a minute," Catlin said.

"You're a skinny bit of nothing, girl. You need your cloak." Fergus grinned suddenly and pounded his chest. "We're big brawny men."

"Big stupid idiots, more like . . ." she said, but she didn't argue further. It *was* cold.

While Fergus worked on the travois and Catlin tried to get a few spoonfuls of broth down Tully's throat, Conor got up and took a tour of the stedding itself. In the clear gray light of the day, the monstrous corpse still slowly roasting on the smoldering bones of the pit looked even more impossible. Breathing through his mouth, Conor leaned close and plucked Tully's dagger from the hound's left eye. The knife came out with a soft, sucking sound, followed by a thick, black sludge that crawled with tiny white maggots. The sight made him suddenly aware of the soup he'd just eaten, and he swallowed hard. Then, gritting his teeth against the nausea, he carefully retrieved Catlin's arrows. There were four. She'd managed to get in quite a few shots, no matter how wild the battle had been.

He nosed around the smithy, but found nothing. The smaller of the two huts was also empty, its dirt floor showing only Catlin's footprints. The larger building was a different matter—he saw sturdy wooden benches, a huge table, and several ancient, crumbling baskets. Everything was larger than a normal man would use, and everything was broken and splintered, as if there'd been a terrific battle here long ago.

He thought of the oversized bones in the firepit. What race of giants had lived in this place? And died? And why did everything in the house look so old, yet the bones still smoldered as if they'd been burned only yesterday?

For a moment his head swam as he stared around. Finally he sighed and shrugged. Another mystery. Some sort of magic. In a way, it was heartening. If you wanted to find magicians, you looked in magical places. This might be just such a place, though the magic had so far not been reassuring.

Myrddin. Only a name, a whisper, recently ghosting down from the north. The northern clans spoke it with awe, though Conor hadn't met anybody who'd actually seen the mysterious sorcerer. There was even a rumor that the magician lived in a glass keep. Conor knew what glass was—he'd seen the milky utensils, made by the Romans, that Diana favored—but he couldn't imagine an entire house made of the stuff. And it was supposed to be perfectly clear, so you could see right through it.

Still musing on this, he kicked aside a pile of junk in one corner of the large room. A cloud of nasty-smelling dust rose up, and he coughed. There was a rotting blanket that crumbled when he touched it, a couple of dry, brittle baskets, half of a cracked wooden bowl, and . . .

He bent down, grunted as his rib protested, but grasped the thing by its shaft and pulled it out.

It came with a sharp, metallic rasp as he dragged it free.

He stood it up and stared at it. A solid iron spear, but like no spear he'd ever seen before. It was of a single piece, shaft and blades, but there were three blades. They all pointed up, something like a wooden hayfork, but this was no farm implement. It was rusted dark red, and on the blades were darker stains. Conor thought there would be a fair amount of work to getting it cleaned up, but it would make a deadly weapon once that was done. He could have used something like it in the battle with the hellhound.

Though he'd never seen such a thing before, he knew what it was. It was called a Gae Bolga, and it was like the weapon Cuchulann himself had used. The spears of the heroes and the High Ones were the same. What was such a thing doing here?

Perhaps this too was an omen. At any rate, it was a weapon, and Conor decided he would take any weapon he could find. He carried it out into the light, where he found Fergus nearly finished with preparing the travois. Fergus stared at the weapon, his gaze suddenly dark.

"Where'd you get that, lad?"

"In the house."

"Maybe you should leave it there . . ."

Conor thought about it, then shook his head. Rusty and stained as it was, it somehow felt good in his hand. As if he was meant to have it.

"You know what it is?" Fergus growled uneasily.

Conor nodded.

"Well, be it on your own head, then." Fergus turned away, shaking his own head and muttering. "Nothing good will come of this . . ."

Half an hour later they were heading north, Fergus and Conor dragging Tully's sleeping form on the travois, Catlin bringing up the rear with an arrow nocked and ready in her bow. They followed what remained of the path. After an hour's slow march, the trail veered away from the stunted woods and arrowed out across a seemingly endless plain of dry stones and sparse gorse.

The deadly stedding vanished behind them. But even though a fitful breeze pushed against their faces from the north, the stench of the dreadful firepit stayed with them most of the rest of the day.

More magic? Conor wondered grimly. If so, it wasn't the sort he was looking for.

I need good magic, he thought. But this is cursed.

—2—

They marched throughout the morning and deep into the afternoon, though at times it seemed as if they hardly moved at all. The sere landscape was unchanging beneath a sky like a sheet of mica, flat and ominously glowing. Every once in a while Fergus would stop and turn over a rock to check for moss; it was the only way he could tell which direction was north.

Conor's belly griped, but he ignored it. There was no use in worrying about it. The land was flat and empty. They saw no sign of spoor, not even rabbits or birds. The earth seemed as dead as the smithy they'd left behind, naked and stripped of all life and hope.

By what they guessed was midday, Tully had developed a fever, and though he didn't wake, now he tossed and groaned in his sleep. They had to stop and tear new strips to tie him to the travois, and so Catlin also lost most of her cloak. With every step, they grew colder and more miserable. Conor began to wonder if he'd finally made a fatal mistake. It was becoming obvious, at least to him, that not only Tully's life was at stake. If they didn't find help, and soon, maybe none of them would make it out of this blasted, unending plain.

Catlin moved up next to Tully and pressed her hand against his brow. "He's getting hotter," she said. "And the edges of his wounds are starting to redden and swell. It will be the rot, if we can't help him soon."

Conor's ribs were a solid, pounding ache. He used the Gae Bolga as a staff with one hand, while holding on to the travois with the other. Nevertheless, his cracked bones were under constant stress. He knew they wouldn't heal quickly, subject to such strains.

Fergus had sunk into a deep, glowering silence, peering out at the land from beneath his ridged brow, his eyes like small, angry animals crouched beneath rocks. By late in the afternoon all of them were trudging wordlessly, concentrating on nothing more than putting one foot in front of the other.

It was Catlin who noticed it first.

"Look, up ahead," she said, her voice raspy and dry.

Dully Conor raised his eyes from the ground in front of him. "What?"

"The horizon. Is it my eyes, or does it look as if the sky is clearing a little there?"

Conor squinted. Yes, she was right. A thin line of blue now stretched along the distant horizon. It was like seeing a rainbow after a storm, full of the light of promise.

"It's there," he said. "You see it, Fergus?"

The old warrior shaded his eyes with his free hand. "Aye," he said. "I see it."

None of them said anything more, but as they marched, their shoulders were a little straighter, their chins a little higher, their eyes a bit brighter.

When dark finally came, they simply lay down in their tracks and slept like the dead. But the last thing they saw before the fall of night was the flashing glimmer of stars far ahead—and the light of the dying sun was clean and bright for the first time in days.

—3—

Conor was walking, the Gae Bolga in his hand shining like freshly minted steel. Overhead burned a moon like a new silver coin tossed onto a field of glittering diamonds. The night was utterly silent, the only movement the glimmering of the countless stars.

Fergus, Catlin, and Tully were nowhere to be seen. He walked alone. The ache in his side was gone. All his aches and pains were gone. He strode with the certainty of a warrior, all fears forgotten. Going somewhere . . .

He blinked, and now, up ahead, he saw the soaring tops of mighty towers. He was only walking, but somehow each stride seemed to cover leagues, for the vast edifice reared above the horizon like a great rising fountain of light. Though all was dark, the castle glowed with its own fire.

He'd once seen an emerald, a Roman stone rudely cut, about the size of the nail on his smallest finger. But when he'd peered into its depths, he'd seen a light like this, pure and green, that had reminded him of the fields of the Land in springtime, fresh and sweet after rain.

From each corner of the mighty pile rose a tower like a curved claw, ending in a point. At the tip of each point gleamed a single star.

He kept marching, feeling the pull of that place like a summons humming deep within his bones. Something waited there for him, something terrible and important, but he didn't know what.

And now, from the four corners of the dark world rose a muttering and a whispering, deep and full like the thunder that presages a storm. In it he could almost, but not quite, detect words.

The sound grew louder, clearer, and he realized it was his own name he heard, over and over again, an insistent call that sent his blood faster and faster through his veins.

Conor . . . Conor . . . *Conor!*

Pain ratcheted through his side.

"Conor, wake *up!*"

"Uh . . . what . . ."

His eyelids felt glued together. It took him a moment of straining to pop them apart. He found himself staring up into Catlin's face, framed against a leaden morning sky. But the quality of the light seemed somehow different.

"Are you all right?" Catlin said. "You were thrashing around and groaning. I thought you'd pull your ribs loose again."

Slowly he sat up. "Ouch! Thanks for waking me up. I was having a dream . . ."

"Not a good one," she said.

He blinked, then rubbed the sleep grit from his eyes. He yawned, and felt his ears pop. "I don't remember," he said. "Morning already."

She leaned back, nodding. "No breakfast, I'm sorry to say. I got up a while ago and went out with my bow, but I didn't see anything." She paused, then said, "Tully's worse. His wounds are swollen, and starting to leak pus. And when I looked at his eyes, one of them is bigger than the other. The dark place in the center."

Conor frowned. He'd seen that sort of thing with head injuries. It was never a good sign.

"Give me a hand," he said, reaching out. She grabbed his wrist and hoisted him up. He brushed bits of broken gorse from his clothes and glanced around. Fergus was crouched over Tully, checking the straps. He looked up, his expression somber.

"He's not good, Conor," he said. "Another day, but no more."

Neither of them mentioned death. But all of them heard the word hanging silently in the morning light, like an invisible, patient specter. Waiting . . .

Conor sighed, then turned his face toward the north. The swatch of blue was wider now, filling nearly a quarter of the sky in that direction. It was like looking out from beneath a filthy gray blanket at a distant light.

"Maybe there," he said wearily. "If the sun is there, perhaps things grow. And where things grow, there must be people."

Fergus stood, dusting his hands together. "We'd best get started, then. As I said, he doesn't have much time." He patted his belly. "Nor do we. Our water won't last forever, and we have no food at all."

He grunted softly. "I'm too old for all this, you know."

For some reason, this struck both Catlin and Conor as hilarious, and both burst out laughing.

"What?" Fergus rumbled.

"You poor old man," Catlin cried. "Poor, ancient old man!"

Fergus glowered at her, but then even he began to grin at his own self-pity, and the dour mood was broken. When they set out a short time later, they walked with a lighter step, and hope gleamed in their eyes.

—4—

Because of the deceptiveness of distances in the gray lands, Conor had been afraid the march might be longer than it looked. But by midday the sky overhead was blue as a robin's egg, and the band of gray was subsiding slowly at their rear.

The earth itself became less stony, softer, more rolling, and here and there patches of green appeared among the gorse. Catlin was ranging out ahead now, bow in hand, searching for game. A half an hour after she'd begun her hunt, Conor saw her raise the bow and draw it. The distant twang of the string sounded pleasantly in his ears, closely followed by Catlin's high shout of triumph. She ran lightly across a hillock, stooped, and raised a fat rabbit.

"Lunch!" she called.

"We might have to eat it raw," Fergus grumbled. But even that didn't sound as bad as it might have. And as it turned out, a few minutes of search turned up enough dry twigs and sticks to make a decent cook-fire. The sun was a hand or so past noon high when Fergus kicked dirt over the smoldering coals and, bellies full, they took up the journey again.

"It's a better land, true enough," Fergus said as they walked along, "but I still don't see any people. Or any magicians."

Yet, though his words were ominous, his expression was not. The breeze from the north had turned soft and warm, and it smelled sweet and full of promise. The stenches they'd suffered for many days now faded away as if they'd never been.

They heard it before they saw it.

"What do you think?" Conor said.

Catlin squinted. "Sounds like water. A river, maybe, or a waterfall."

Conor nodded. "Up ahead . . ."

They walked another hour or so, the land rising steadily beneath their feet, until they reached a crest and looked down on a broad valley that opened out toward the west.

This declivity was so wide, its limits were lost in golden mists and sunlight. A river meandered down the center, and curved away into the distance on either side. Perhaps not a valley, Conor thought, but a great island beyond.

The valley was covered with rich grassland interspersed with broad patches of forest. Their path would bring them down to the east of the river. Conor squinted: Something glinted brightly beyond the river, though he couldn't quite make out what it was.

The only odd thing about this entrancing vista was at the foot of the rise on which they stood—a swirl of fog that clung to the land, obscuring whatever was behind it. But their path to the river did not approach this spot. Some kind of swamp, Conor thought, and then forgot about it.

"If those fields aren't stuffed with game, I'll chew the grass myself," Fergus announced happily. "You'll try my chicken soup yet!" He paused. "Well, maybe pigeon, but you won't be able to tell the difference!"

Laughing, they took up the travois and continued down. Two hours later, as the afternoon began to shade into a soft purple dusk, they reached the river.

By the time Fergus had kindled a fire, Catlin returned with a brace of fat rabbits and the largest duck Conor had ever seen.

"We feast tonight!" she announced, holding out her trophies. Fergus's grin ran from one jug ear to the other. "There's water tubers down along the river bank. Something to flavor our meat!"

It was a wonderful moment, and it held for almost ten seconds before Tully awoke and began to scream.

# THREE

## THE LAND OF APPLES

—1—

"Tully!" Catlin cried as they all scrambled to his side. His face was ruddy with fever, his eyes wide, the left eye seeming to bulge slightly. The pupil of that eye was so large it nearly filled the socket, leaving only a thin, yellow-white ring around the edge.

She knelt next to him and touched his forehead. He didn't seem to see her, but he flinched away.

"He's burning up!" she said. "Conor, soak your shirt in the river and bring it to me."

Conor did as he was bid. Thankfully, the day was still warm. He squeezed out the excess water and handed the shirt to Catlin, who draped it across Tully's brow. "Tully . . ." she said softly. "Can you hear me?"

The boy moaned softly. His lips were scabbed where the cracks had bled.

Conor and Fergus glanced at each other. Catlin might still have hope, but the two men knew they were looking at death, and the madness that sometimes comes just before death.

"Tully . . ." Catlin said again.

*"Not the river!"* Tully screamed suddenly. *"Don't cross the river!"* He began to thrash about.

"Help me!" Catlin said as she threw herself across his writhing body. Fergus and Conor added their weight. Tully's muscles, tense with the strength of insanity, felt like a bag of snakes inside his dry, wasted skin.

After a few moments, his spurious strength drained away and he settled back, exhausted. Catlin lifted his shirt and checked his wounds. They were black with poison. Tears glittered on her cheeks as she stared across him at the others.

"He's dying, isn't he?" she said.

Nobody said anything. Then Fergus sighed heavily. "Yes, lass, he is."

"We have to *do* something! Why can't either of you *help* him?"

Conor reached across Tully's supine form and took her hand. He could feel the heat baking off the youth beneath him like the glow from a banked oven.

"You have your Roman god," he said gently. "Maybe you could pray to him . . ."

Catlin nodded. "Yes, I will. Of course I will. But isn't there anything else . . . ?"

Conor looked at her, then at Tully. "I'm going to cross the river," he said. "The magician must live there. I'll find him, and bring him back."

Fergus made a soft choking sound. "The boy might be mad, but it may be the madness of prophecy, Conor. He said not to cross."

"What other chance do we have? What do you want me to do? Just sit here and wait for him to *die?*"

Fergus didn't have an answer. At least, none he liked well enough to voice. He shook his head sadly, stood up, and walked back to his cookery. Conor and Catlin stared at each other.

"Do it, Conor," she said finally. "I can't think of anything else. It may be useless, but it's all we have." She looked down. "All he has . . ."

Conor nodded, and stood up. The muscles ridging his naked back gleamed in the fading light of the day. The bruises on his ribs stood out like patches of ink.

"I'll go now," he said. "There's not much sun left."

She nodded. Conor stood up, glanced down at her, then walked over to Fergus and squatted.

"I'm going to swim across," he said quietly.

"A fool's errand, boy," Fergus replied, but he also kept his voice low. "You don't even know what you're looking for. How do you expect to find it?"

Conor lowered his eyes. "At this point, I don't know that I expect to find anything," he said. "But I have to try. Tully's my friend. Can you think of anything else that offers any hope?"

Fergus poked at the roasting duck, then looked up and shook his head.

"Right," Conor said. "Well, then. You stay

here, keep watch. If anybody shows up, just shout for me as loud as you can. I don't know where I'll be, but if I hear you, I'll come back as fast as I'm able."

Fergus nodded. "The High Ones speed you, lad. And watch over your back, since I won't be able to."

He extended one huge, gnarled hand. Conor took it and squeezed. There was nothing more to say. Conor stood up without another word and walked silently to the edge of the river.

The afternoon light seemed brighter on the other side. In the distance, he heard the sound of birdsong, high and sweet.

Like a miracle.

—2—

Conor dropped to his haunches and dabbled his fingers in the swiftly flowing water. It felt pleasantly cool, but not cold. The current was steady, rushing from his right to his left, but not so strong that it would sweep him far downriver.

At this point the water was about twenty paces wide. Despite having grown up near the shore of the sea, Conor knew he wasn't the strongest swimmer ever born, but he judged he would be able to get across. Assuming there were no hidden currents out toward the middle . . .

He realized he was letting his thoughts wander, putting off the necessity of action. Why? Had Tully's screams been anything more than the ravings of fever?

A faint chill prickled his back. He stood, kicked off his boots, unbuckled his sword, and set it carefully on the grass. The water made a soft, pervasive hissing sound as it hurried past. He stared at it, took a breath, closed his eyes, and half dived, half fell into its powerful embrace.

He came up blowing and splashing, thrashed around a moment, then began to stroke toward the far banks using a crude but effective dog paddle. He knew he could keep that up for a long time, but it turned out not to be necessary. There seemed to be no tricky currents to slow him down, and the general current was even gentler than he'd hoped. It swept him slowly sideways as his course cut against its flow. After no more than forty or fifty strokes, he felt his knees bump against a gravel bottom. He got his feet under him, stood, and waded the final few feet to the shore. A moment later he stood on a soft, thick carpet of grass, water dripping off him, his wet hair in his eyes. He brushed it away, turned, and looked back across the river.

Fergus and Catlin stood watching him. The light there was strange, somehow darker. It looked as if they stood in shadow. He waved, and heard their thin cries of response. They sounded much farther away than just the breadth of the water. He shook his head. Maybe his ears were plugged from the swim . . .

He gave a final wave, then turned around to get his bearings. As soon as he did so, he realized why the far shore had seemed so oddly illuminated. The light *was* different here. In fact . . .

Overhead, the sun rode serenely at the very apex of the sky, a great white flare of light, its rays touching his back with a gentle warmth that loosened his muscles and filled him with a kind of pleasure he'd never felt before.

But it was the sun of high noon, and on the other side of the river dusk was approaching. Surely that was impossible. Before this strangeness could unsettle him further, a fat bumblebee came looping past his nose, its wings whirring softly. And with that, he abruptly heard the myriad songs of robins, bluebirds, nightingales, and nameless others. The boughs of the great oaks were full of them, clouds of color drifting from canopy to canopy, singing.

The oaks loomed over him, their ancient hides seeming to glow with a golden inner light. The turf beneath his bare toes felt less like earth and more like a soft bed, inviting him to lie on it and take his rest. He suddenly thought that, even without boots, he could trek for miles across these grasses and never feel the slightest weariness.

The air throbbed with magic. He took a step and felt his ribs mutter in protest, and that brought him out of what seemed like a dream. His bruised, aching ribs were real enough. And so was Tully, dying on the far shore.

He raised his head and looked around. There was nothing to indicate a likely direction. Everything was beautiful, and possessed a purity that seemed to hint this place had never been despoiled by the touch of man or woman, had instead been kept pristine and shining from the moment of its creation.

Truly a wondrous world, but . . . no magician. And no hint of one. Yet none of this worried him much. It was as if the very air he breathed soothed away his fears. The light that warmed his shoulders cooled his mind. And as he stood there, trying to decide, the breeze shifted, and he smelled apples.

He sniffed. Yes, apples without a doubt, but a scent unlike anything he'd ever before known. Crisp and fresh, as much a taste as a smell, and a far cry from the small, wrinkled orbs stored away in baskets for the winter that he was used to.

Suddenly his mouth began to water and he felt a ravenous, irresistible hunger. The stand of oaks was to his left, the tip of a vast arrow-point of woods that touched the vein of the river. But to his right the land sloped softly upward, and in the distance he saw a darker, lower line of trees. Was it only his imagination, or did he also see, gleaming among those green boughs, tiny red globes?

Without another thought he set off toward the beckoning orchard, barely noticing a huge rabbit that sat up on its white haunches and eyed him without fear as he hurried past. The grasses were as soft and comforting as he'd imagined. No stone bruised his heel, no nettle scraped his skin. It seemed that barely an instant passed before he found himself standing beneath the broad, spreading limbs of the largest apple tree he'd ever seen.

High above his head a massive bough arched down, so laden with ruby-tinted fruit it seemed it must break and dump its load onto the ground at any moment. Yet there were no fallen apples beneath this tree, or any other. The grass was unmarked and empty.

The perfume filled his nose and dizzied him. He couldn't deny his hunger any longer. Without thought he bent his knees and jumped, extending his arm straight up. His fingertips just brushed the skin of the lowest fruit and he fell back, a groan of agony wrung from his throat. His ribs were suddenly on fire.

He took a deep, ragged breath, gritted his teeth, and leaped again. This time his fingers closed on the fruit and pulled it free. It tumbled into his hands as he fell back. Ignoring the blaze in his side, he raised it to his face. The apple was huge, as large as his two fists together. Its skin felt cool and warm at the same time, and looked translucent—as if he could see into its depths like some murky jewel.

He closed his eyes as he bit into it. The skin parted with a sharp, clean snap. Then the meat of it, and its nectar, filled his mouth.

The juice that poured down his throat was thick as honey and as sweet, yet tempered with a sharp, bright aftertaste, like the best spring wine he'd ever tasted. It filled his mind with memories of childhood, when everything had been golden, and the sadness and cares of manhood far away.

He ate the apple in a frenzy of chewing, until suddenly he was holding only its gnawed core. He stared at the ordered rows of dark seeds, thinking vaguely that they looked more like small, perfect gems than anything from which a tree might grow.

He let the core tumble from his fingers and then, still hungry for the taste of those fruits, he leaped up again. This time he bounded into the air as if his legs were those of a giant. It seemed that if he wished, he might jump clear over the tops of the trees. Maybe even fly . . .

Sometime later the haze of hunger and fulfillment finally abated, and he found himself standing beneath the tree, a circle of gnawed apple cores around him, his belly sated as it had never been before.

His ribs no longer ached.

He looked down. The bruises that had been so livid before were gone, his skin now pale and milky, as if renewed to the softness of a babe's. Wondering, he touched himself. No pain, none at all. His ribs felt whole and solid. In fact, everything about him felt rested and renewed, as if he'd just awakened from a long, deep slumber and eaten the finest meal in the world.

If this is magic, he thought, then give me more of it.

He stepped out from beneath the tree and looked up at the sky. His body told him that time had passed. He had the feeling that a *lot* of time had passed. But the sun still rode the noon-arc, centered directly above. He blinked.

Then he pulled off his breeks and stood naked for a moment, luxuriating in the warmth and light. He felt no shame. Somehow, in this place, nakedness was natural, even desirable.

He stretched, long and lazily. Then he picked up his pants, went back to the tree, and began to leap up, again and again, until he had enough. He thought that perhaps one would do, but he wanted to be absolutely certain.

—3—

Conor stuffed the seat of his pants with apples, then pulled his belt tight to make a queer sort of sack for them. As he walked back toward the river, he tied the legs of his trews around his neck. He walked several paces against the current, keeping his eye on the location of his friends across the water, and finally slipped back into the gentle current. To his surprise, the air trapped in his makeshift bag buoyed him up. He crossed without incident, climbing up the grassy bank almost directly in front of Catlin, who stared at his nakedness and grinned.

"You need some meat on those bones, Conor. You look like a chicken leg."

He blushed, and one hand strayed palm-wide toward his middle, and she laughed out loud at that. Then, suddenly, she sobered.

"What happened to your ribs? The bruises—they're gone."

Conor untied his dripping breeks, opened the belt, and spilled the apples out onto the ground. "It's magic," he said. "I ate apples from a tree over there, and suddenly my ribs were healed."

He looked down at the softly glowing red fruits. "I'm hoping they will do the same for Tully."

Her gaze flicked from the apples on the ground to Conor's ribs and back again, her eyes slowly growing wide. "Magic apples," she breathed.

"Magic what?" Fergus grumbled as he walked over. He didn't miss much. He saw the change to Conor's wounds immediately. "What happened, boy?"

When Conor finished explaining, Fergus's unsettlement was written plainly on his blunt features. "I don't like it," he said finally, shaking his head. "Magic. Magic's always a knife that cuts two ways . . ." Then he turned, and glanced at Tully's unconscious form. "But he's dying, and if . . ."

He shook his head again. "Try it. Even if it kills him, well . . . he's not far from that now."

Conor picked up an apple and offered it to Catlin. "Try it."

"No, thank you." She took it, though, and stared at it thoughtfully. "We can't just ram this down his throat, you know. He's knocked out. Can't chew anything."

He closed his eyes. "Can we mash it up somehow? I don't see how it would make a difference whether he chewed or not, if we can just get it into him. Maybe make a paste and mix it with some water, see if we can get him to swallow it that way?"

"It's worth a try," Catlin said.

They found a couple of smooth, flat stones, and pulverized one of the apples between them. Catlin said the smell that arose from the crushed meat reminded her of a flower garden, or a bucket of honey. A smile grew slowly on her features as she worked.

When they had a quantity of the sweet-smelling mush, Conor mixed a bite or two of it with water in his palm.

"Hold his head up," he told her.

She settled to the ground cross-legged and moved Tully's head into her lap. He gave no sign of any awareness, and when Conor placed his palm next to Tully's lips, they didn't move.

"He's not taking it," Conor said after the third try.

"Do it again. I'll pinch his nose. He'll have to open up to breathe."

In this manner they managed to get a few tastes of their gruel into Tully's mouth. One he coughed up, splattering them, but they saw his throat work as he swallowed.

"Some of it's going down," he said.

Then they waited.

— 4 —

"It's not working," she said.

Conor sighed and shook his head. "No. It happened fast with me, almost as soon as I ate the apple." He paused, then said uncertainly, "At least I *think* it did . . ."

She glanced up at the sun. It was now sinking toward the west. "You were only gone a few minutes."

He followed the direction of her gaze. "You know, I don't remember the sun moving at all on the other side of the river. It always seemed like it was high noon . . . so I guess I don't really know how long it took."

Catlin wiped a thin line of half-dried fruit mush from the corner of Tully's mouth. His lips moved faintly, then became still again.

"Maybe it only works on you . . ."

Conor thought about it, then got up, and returned a moment later with another apple. "We can find out. You try it. You've got a few bruises yourself."

"No, I . . ." She stared at the apple, then reached forward suddenly. "All right. At least we'll know for sure." But her hand trembled slightly as she brought the apple to her lips. She paused one breath, then bit deeply into the succulent skin. Conor watched her, waiting, as she chewed.

"Well . . . ?"

But she didn't answer. She was too busy pushing the rest of the apple through her teeth as fast as she could chew. Juice dripped from her chin. She wiped it with her palm, then licked her hand clean.

"That's the best thing I've ever tasted," she said.

Conor stared at her, his own disappointment a sad counterpoint to the look of glowing pleasure on her face. "Yes, but you still have that big bruise on your neck."

She reached up, put a finger at the side of her neck, and winced. "Still hurts too."

They waited a while, but nothing changed. The apples were delicious, but they seemed no longer to have any healing effect.

"They must only work over there," Conor said finally. "I could feel a magic in the air . . . and the sun didn't move." He looked back toward the river. As dusk pressed harder, purple shadows stretched across the rippling surface of the water.

"We'll have to take Tully over there. Across the river."

At that, Tully gave another moan, and his face twisted as if he might begin to scream again. But he subsided after a moment. They stared at him.

"He's dying, Catlin. We have to try."

Fergus, sitting a few paces away, had been silent, but now he spoke: "How do you propose to get him across the river, Conor? He's deadweight. Even if you and I can hold on to him, we're likely to drown him by accident."

Conor thought about the way the air trapped in his pants had buoyed him before. He grinned. "We'll float him across," he said. "The first thing you need to do is take off your pants."

Fergus didn't stop roaring for nearly five minutes, and it took another ten to actually get him out of his breeks. Nor did it help any that after he'd made the ultimate sacrifice, Catlin's cheeks turned the color of strawberries and she began to stifle small giggles every few moments.

As Conor carefully lowered Tully, two pairs of trousers tied around his neck, into Fergus's waiting arms, the old warrior glared up at him. "I've made a lot of sacrifices for you in my time, boy"— he grunted as he took Tully's weight—"but this is the worst. Naked as a jay. It's no way for a man to face things."

Conor slipped into the water beside him and took Tully's other arm. "Oh, quit your griping. You act as if you have something worth hiding . . ."

Fergus glared at him. "Hide. That's a good word. As soon as we get across, I believe I'll have me some of yours. As soon as I strip it from your bones with my bare hands."

"Huh. Not the only thing bare about you . . ."

Fergus snorted. They set off. Catlin followed them, a third makeshift airbag helping to buoy up their swords, bows, and spears—including Conor's Gae Bolga. It was heavy, and dangerous to carry across the water. But something told him he would need it for more than knocking enchanted apples from magical trees.

—5—

It took a bit of struggling, and once, Tully nearly slipped from their grasp, but finally they mounted the far bank, carrying his limp body between them. They laid him down on the grass. Fergus stood, shaded his eyes, and gazed back across the water.

"Getting dark over there . . ."

Conor looked up. Overhead, the sun hung suspended like a great lamp, exactly at the pinnacle of the sky. Fergus nodded. "Magic. More magic than I ever thought I'd see." Suddenly, though the air was warm, he shivered. "Run and get your apples, lad. We came for a reason, not to gawk."

Conor nodded, then moved down the bank and gave Catlin a hand as she scrambled up the verge. He unwrapped the Gae Bolga and set off with it over his shoulder, and carrying one of the cloaks they'd used to wrap Tully in. It was so pleasant here, Conor doubted Tully would miss the makeshift blankets.

He returned within a short while, laden with fruit. Catlin again prepared a mush, and they fed it to the unconscious boy. His jaws worked slowly as he swallowed. Catlin and Fergus squatted around him, watching Conor as he held his hand to Tully's mouth.

Suddenly Tully's head moved forward. His eyes were still closed, but now he licked Conor's hand. Conor could feel his tongue scrape frantically against his palm as Tully sought every tiny scrap.

"Give me an apple," Conor said softly. Catlin handed one over. Conor put the whole fruit against Tully's lips. Fergus grunted as the boy opened his mouth and bit cleanly through the crisp skin.

Tully opened his eyes. "More," he said.

Catlin burst into tears.

—6—

"I don't remember anything, not even the big dog," Tully was saying. They had moved away from the river, toward the hem of the oaken forest, and now sat on soft grass with their backs against bark that glowed like hand-polished wood. The sweet smell of wildflowers floated in the air. Sunbeams drifted through the softly rustling canopy overhead, so that the earth was dappled with translucent coins of buttery light.

Tully stared at them in bemused wonderment.

"You say I've been asleep for days? And that I was wounded?" As he spoke, he looked down at his belly. Only a few smooth, pale marks remained of the terrible, polluted wounds from the hellhound's claws. And his skull, which had been lopsided from the swelling, now showed no sign of any damage. His eyes were bright and clear.

Though everybody was dressed, more or less, only Catlin wore a shirt. The temperature, even in the green shade beneath the trees, was as warm as a perfect summer day.

Tully ran his fingertips across the fading remnants of his wounds. Even as they watched, these lighter patches were smoothing and growing darker. Soon they would be gone, invisible.

"I guess I have to believe you," Tully said. "But—I'm supposed to be a magician. You say apples did this? That was all, nothing more?"

"What do you mean?" Conor asked.

"No chants? No spells or potions or rituals? No hocus-pocus, just apples?"

Conor nodded.

"Healing magic is some of the hardest," Tully said slowly. "Galen taught me that. You thought of him as a sorcerer, a wizard, and he was all of that, and more—but I knew him better. He was really a healer, because that was what he wanted most. He knew more about healing than anybody I've ever heard of—and still, he lost one of every two he tried to help." Tully paused, and once again, almost unconsciously, his fingers traced the path of his wounds. "Healing isn't easy. If it was as you say, Conor, these apples are mighty magic. So powerful, in fact, there is only one thing they could be."

Catlin leaned forward. "What do you mean?"

Tully lifted his head and stared at her. "The Island of Apples. Avallon. And we've eaten the Apples of Avallon. All of us."

"Not me," Fergus rumbled suddenly. "I don't eat magic apples." Then what Tully said hit him, and he froze. "Avallon?" he breathed at last.

Tully nodded. "Avallon. The Isle of the Sidhe."

His words sank hooks of ice into Conor's spine. His lips moved, shaping the impossible words: "The home of the gods . . ."

"Exactly," Tully said.

# FOUR

## DREAMS OF THE SIDHE

—1—

They talked for a long time, or so it seemed. More and more, Conor was coming to understand that time was a slippery idea in this strange place. Though they spoke for what he was certain was many hours, the sun never moved, nor did the light change. Twice they saw animals; once, a rabbit with fur so white it looked freshly washed, and later, a fearless doe with eyes like amber.

When the deer appeared, wandering boldly between the trees, paying them no attention, Catlin reached for her bow and began to lift it.

"No," Conor said softly. "Don't harm it."

"We could use some meat," she replied, equally hushed. "It will be a long journey back."

"I think it would be a cursed act to murder anything that lives in this place. Besides, we won't starve. I could eat those apples forever."

She kept her eyes on the doe, which continued to ignore her as it stepped daintily past them and finally vanished into the woods beyond, but she put down her weapon. "I'm not sure I could kill a beast so beautiful and so fearless," she said.

"You may not starve, but I haven't eaten your apples, Conor," Fergus said after the deer was gone. "And I won't. They're magic, and magic is perilous."

"And still magic," Catlin broke in. "Look at Tully."

Fergus nodded, his expression dour. "I see him. But everything has a price. That's one of the first things you learn about sorcery. Isn't that right, Tully?"

Tully's eyelids flickered. "In magic, there must always be a balance," he said finally. "But that doesn't always necessarily mean . . ."

"Aye, spare me your weasel words, boy. *Always,* and *necessarily.* You left out *perhaps* and *maybe.* But I heard the word *must* clear enough. You didn't weasel that one. And I know what it means. It means there's a payback for everything."

He turned his head and spat, then nodded, pleased with himself. "Magical payback. Not so much different than the real world."

"Grumpy old man," Conor said, half laughing. "See the bad side of everything. Somebody gives you a horse, I'll bet you check its teeth . . ."

Fergus stared at him, his eyebrows rising. "Well, of course I would. Wouldn't you?"

Conor knew when he'd been gaffed for fair, and let the subject drop. So Fergus was a stubborn, cranky old man. That was surely no surprise.

Eventually the conversation began to lag, and finally failed entirely. Tully was the first to fade away, his eyes slowly closing until Catlin noticed he wasn't answering her anymore. Fergus went next, though with less subtlety. He simply dropped his chin onto his chest, opened his mouth, and began to snore like a sty full of disgruntled hogs.

Catlin grinned at the two of them, then at Conor. "Tully has good reason to be tired, and Fergus is the oldest among us. But I'm not tired, Conor. What about you?"

Conor shook his head. "Fresh as a blooming rose," he said. "I feel like I could get up and run."

"Me too." She stretched. "But maybe they have the right idea. We don't know what may come, and maybe it would be better to be rested when we do finally meet it." Her gaze slid away. "Whatever it turns out to be . . ."

Conor wondered if he could sleep even if he wanted to, but there was wisdom in what Catlin said. It was the first thing any good soldier learned: to sleep—and eat—whenever you could. You never knew when you might have to go days without either.

Oddly enough, though he felt relaxed and full of energy, as soon as Catlin spoke of sleep, he found himself yawning. He stretched. Out of habit, he winced as the muscles along his rib cage expanded, but there was no pain, nor the slightest bit of tightness.

"I don't know if I can sleep," he said.

"Close your eyes and try counting sheep . . ." Catlin said.

"Sheep? Those nasty, stinking beasts? I'd rather count . . . oh, I don't know. Apples, maybe."

"Yes," she said. "Apples. Apples would be good . . ."

"Apples . . ." he replied, his voice suddenly thick with drowsiness.

She didn't hear him. She was asleep. A moment later, so was he. After a little while, the doe returned, stepping with finicky elegance through the center of their little camp. She didn't turn aside, didn't even slow. She paid them no more attention than she did rock or leaf.

Almost as if they weren't there at all.

—2—

Conor opened his eyes to a trail of white clouds drifting slowly across the sun. He blinked. The world was full of a breathless silence. He lifted his head, feeling himself filled with a preternatural awareness. He could hear the sounds of his own body, its tiny stretching and creakings suddenly loud in his ears.

"What?" he whispered.

He pushed himself up on his elbows, feeling the springy give of the green turf beneath him, as soft as the finest bed. He looked around, his gaze caught for a moment in a net of still, perfect beauty.

Everything he saw shimmered, as if it had been dusted with light. He was overcome with so strong a feeling of strangeness that for a moment he thought he might cry out in fear . . . or just cry.

In that strangled instant he thought of his father, and his father's death. And his mother too; had she screamed as she died? Had she fought?

Or had she gone quietly?

Catlin slept before him, curled gently on her side, one finger resting against the corner of her lips. Just beyond her, Tully lay with his elbows pressed against his knees, his belly hidden inside the curl of him, the light tickling his hair.

Fergus sprawled to the right, legs spread, flat on his back, one hand across his heart as in a pledge. He snored, huge grating sounds full of wind and wet, his upper lip vibrating, his mustache like some small frightened animal riding a fleshy earthquake.

Conor saw and felt all this in the one crystalline moment of awaking and arising into a world pregnant with light and mystery. For the first time, he felt the utter strangeness of everything—not just here, in this place, but in the world he'd left. He had by choice taken certain paths, no matter how much he might have protested his fate. But fate had offered only the opportunity for choice. He had taken it, and made the choices, and those choices had led him here.

"Catlin . . ." he said. Then, "Catlin!"

He bent his knees beneath him, then his feet, and stumbled toward her, uncertain whether he moved through a dream, uncertain whether it mattered.

"Catlin!"

The skin across her cheekbone was smooth and cool, hard as fine porcelain, faintly dented with the impression of her fingertip. His own fingernail gave off a faint click as he touched her.

"Catlin?"

His voice sounded muffled and thick in his own ears. He left her for a moment, because to do so was to leave, at least temporarily, a horror that stretched far beyond his feeble mind, that choked his silent inward screams with bands of thorns.

Tully was coiled like a worm in silence, unmoving, pristine, unreachable though not untouchable. His flesh did not move beneath Conor's hands. Conor felt his jaws creak. He knew he must be shouting something, though he could no longer hear the sound of his own voice, nor could he understand the shrill, wordless keening of his thoughts.

He saw Fergus shake and shudder awake, saw the old, gnarled warrior leap to his feet with unnatural grace, saw the silver flame of Fergus's greatsword come sliding from its scabbard like the tongue of a snake, questing and deadly.

"What! What is it, lad?"

Conor stared up at him. "They are stone," he said simply. "They've turned to stone."

—3—

At first Fergus didn't understand. He stood irresolute, the point of his sword slowly dropping, his bald head swiveling back and forth. "Stone?" he said. "What are you talking about?"

Conor had been crouching over Tully. Now he

brought his hand down on the frozen youth's shoulder. The sound that issued forth was not that of flesh on flesh, but of skin on stone.

"What . . . ?" Fergus said.

Conor's features twisted in sudden anguish. "My fault!" he cried. "I brought him here! And her! Across that cursed river."

Fergus sheathed his sword. He stumbled over, his knees knocking together, and squatted next to Conor. He ran trembling fingertips across the glassy surface of Tully's cheek. As he touched that cool, inhuman surface, his expression crumpled, and he jerked his hand away in terror and disgust.

"Ahh, what has happened? Are they dead?"

His question broke the malign stasis that had descended on Conor's own thoughts. He took a long breath, then looked across at Catlin.

"I don't know," he said. "It must be a spell of some kind. Magic. And spells can be reversed, or broken . . ."

"Magic . . ." Fergus echoed, but in his tone was all the loathing he'd already expressed. "I knew no good could come of it."

Conor's own pain was still evident. He bowed his head. "Yes, you were right. And I was wrong. I . . . can you forgive me, Fergus?" He raised his face, and Fergus saw his tears. "Can they forgive me?"

Fergus shook his head, clearly without an answer. For a long moment they both remained motionless, pressed beneath the weight of this fresh disaster. Finally Conor sniffed, wiped his nose across the back of his arm, and stood up. He looked around, blinking, as if he were seeing his surroundings for the first time.

"It was the apples," he said at last. "They ate them, and you didn't."

But Fergus shook his head. "Nay, lad," he said softly, "you ate them too."

Fear flickered in Conor's eyes. "Then maybe I will become as they are."

"You ate first, Conor. If it's the apples, you should have been the first to go." Fergus shivered. "And I would have awakened alone . . ."

A flicker of movement off to their left, deeper in the trees, brought them both around. The doe paused in her passage, amber eyes glinting, and stared at them. Then, with a flick of her ears, she vanished. They stared at each other.

"I hate this place!" Fergus said. "That doe—it was almost as if she knew what had happened here."

Conor nodded slowly. "Perhaps she does. I think that spirits are in all things here." He looked down at Tully, then at Catlin. "We have to get them back across the river, Fergus. It may be the spell only works on this side of the water. Like the apples."

Fergus stared at Conor, then at Tully's motionless form. "I'll be glad to put this wizard's isle at my back," he muttered. "But at what cost?"

He bent over, took Tully by his shoulders, and, grunting, tried to shift him.

"Ungh! He weighs as much as if he were a stone." Tully, rigid, had moved only slightly. "It will take the both of us, Conor, and even then it won't be easy."

Conor nodded, shading his eyes with his palm as he measured the distance from their camp to the hazy, far-off line of the river.

"It may be hard, but what else can we do?" He sighed, and dusted his hands on his flanks. Half under his breath, he said, "And if we can find that wizard . . ."

But Fergus glared at him and roared, "Spare me your damned wizards, boy. Haven't you caused enough trouble already with your seeking?"

Conor had no answer to that. The evidence of its truth lay at his feet, silent, immobile, and obdurate. He looked up at the sun. It hadn't moved.

They set to work.

—4—

It was almost impossible to measure time in this place—if indeed time existed here at all. Conor wondered about that. All he knew was that they slept three times before they finally brought their friends to the edge of the river. And here they halted, because the question both of them had avoided throughout their backbreaking labors now stared them in the face, and they could not evade it any longer.

Fergus, sweat gleaming on his shining dome, stared across the slowly moving water. On the other side, the light seemed different, as if dawn were just rising to paint the grasses with pink and silver.

"How do we get them across?"

The question was simple, but not so any answer. Their backs, arms, and legs ached from dragging the stony weights across the grass. Only with the greatest effort, working together, had they been able to lift either Tully or Catlin off the ground, and they couldn't hold them for long. Mostly they'd just dragged them by their feet, their friends' immobile heads carving a trail on the turf. At first this method seemed disrespectful, but there was no other way. Conor finally consoled himself with the idea that Tully and Catlin must be senseless of anything outside the spell that held them, though he pushed the thought quickly away. It led to another: What *were* they seeing, hearing, thinking in their flinty dreams?

"We can barely lift them. How can we float them across the water?" Fergus continued. "They'll end up in the mud on the bottom of the river."

Conor sighed and nodded. "I know."

"And that's all? You don't have any other ideas?"

Conor shook his head.

Fergus looked at the two frozen figures. "Then we have dragged them a long ways to bury them."

"What? Bury them?"

"What else, Conor? We can't get them across the water. We can't just leave them here. There may be things more fell than rabbits and does in the forest. Magical things, perhaps, that can gnaw on magical bones and flesh." He shook his head. "They're gone, lad. We can't help them, except to protect their remnant from desecration. Bury them deep, where nothing can disturb them . . ."

But Conor was staring at him in horror. "Bury them? Fergus, *think!* This is a spell. Sometimes spells just wear off. What if these did? And they awoke, just as they had been, but . . ."

Fergus grimaced and turned away, his palm going to his mouth. After a moment he spat. His lips worked again, but his mouth had gone dry.

"We must have hope, Fergus!" Conor said. "I won't give up!"

"Aye, lad. And so what will you do? It seems to me you've done enough already."

Conor flinched as if Fergus had struck him. But his eyes blazed defiantly, though his cheeks colored. "If that's the way you feel, you may be right. I said this was all my fault. But I won't desert them. I won't give up! I'll keep on trying until—"

"Until you die? Until the Alliance falls apart in ruins? Until everything your father dreamed of, and you've worked for, is utterly destroyed? Is that how long?"

"Ahh . . . Fergus."

The older man stepped toward him, relenting of his anger. He put his hand on Conor's shoulder. "It isn't an easy decision, Conor. I know it feels like a betrayal, to just leave them like this. But what would they want you to do? They've worked to build the Alliance too. They came with you, knowing of the risks, because they wanted to save the Alliance." He paused, took a deep breath, and continued. "Imagine that they lay before you now, not as they are, but with spears through their hearts. Dead. What would you do then?"

Tears glittered on Conor's cheeks again. "I'd . . . I would . . ." He couldn't go on. He turned away.

"Yes. You would bury them, and commend their spirits to their gods, and go on. That's what you would do, and now that's what you must do."

Conor dropped to his knees, his hands seeking, and finding, the stony, rigid flesh of his friends. But he found no warmth, nor any hope, and after a long moment he looked up.

"Maybe . . . you are right."

"I am," Fergus whispered.

*"Ho, the island . . ."* a voice cried thinly.

—5—

A strange, weak fog had begun to drift in tendrils along the opposite bank of the river, so that the figure standing there was partly obscured behind its nebulous veils. Nevertheless, Conor could make our a shape that seemed small, perhaps even bent, leaning on a tall staff. The figure was cloaked and hooded in gray, his face hidden; yet Conor sensed a strength there, a certain power, though somehow masked.

He knew the feeling. He had felt it with Galen, and to some extent with the young Blas. The only other he'd ever known who possessed magic was Longinus, but with that one neither his power nor his malevolence was so much concealed as flaunted.

He cupped his hands around his mouth and shouted back: "Who are you? What do you want?"

There came a moment of silence, and then, more strongly than before, a reply. "I am Myrddin, Conor. I am the one you seek."

Fergus uttered a strangled groan. "Just what we need. More damned magic."

"Fergus . . ."

"Lad, give off. Don't you understand? Four of us set out, and only two remain. Maybe that was this wizard's doing. You are a fool if you take this further. Mark my words, and turn away from this!"

Conor could hear a faint tremor in Fergus's voice, and knew with a kind of wonder that the mighty warrior, fearless veteran of a hundred battles, was terrified. Well, there is no dishonor in that, he thought, as his gaze strayed to his silent friends at his feet. If I had paid Fergus's fears more heed, perhaps we wouldn't find ourselves in such dire need now.

But I didn't, and we do, he thought. "Wait, Fergus," he said softly. "Maybe he can help us."

Fergus eyed him darkly, then shook his head, turned, and stomped away from the riverbank. "Be it on your own head, then," he said. "I'll have nothing to do with it."

Conor watched him go, feeling an unaccustomed flare of irritation kindle inside himself. By the gods and spirits! They all wanted him to lead, expected him to lead, but when he tried to do so, all he got was naysaying. What did they expect? What did *Fergus* expect? Could *he* have done any better?

So it was that Conor wrestled with the oldest conundrum of the leader as he turned again to the bank, and maybe this made his voice louder, more defiant, than it had been before.

"I am Conor, Derek's Son. If you are Myrddin, as you say, then come to me across the water. I cannot leave my friends."

"Nor can I cross the river, Conor," came the reply. "I am barred from the Isle of Apples. If you wish my help, you must come to me, for I cannot come to you."

"Right," Fergus muttered. "There's your all-powerful wizard, Conor. Can't even swim across a little stream. Maybe he's afraid he'll get his hems wet."

"It's hardly a little stream," Conor replied. "And from here, Myrddin looks to be an old man." He grinned slyly. "Older, even, than you."

Fergus whirled. "What do you mean, old? I can beat you across that puddle any day of the week. With one hand tied behind me."

Conor laughed out loud. "Then do it, old man!" And with that he dived cleanly into the water and began to paddle for the opposite bank.

—6—

Conor came out dripping and blowing, to find himself facing a hooded shape nearly his own height.

"Well met, Conor, son of Derek," Myrddin said. His voice was soft, but thrummed with power nonetheless. "Shake yourself dry, and then we will talk."

With that he stepped away, and waited for Conor to compose himself. Conor flung his head back and forth, sending off a shower of glittering drops. He did not notice that the magician was careful to avoid even a touch of that water. He turned at the sound of splashing behind him, and saw Fergus arrive at the bank in a flail of arms and a chorus of splutters. Grinning, he reached down, grabbed Fergus's wrist, and yanked him from the river.

"Beat me, will you?"

"You tricked me. It wasn't a fair start!"

"Well met, Fergus, King's Hand," Myrddin said, and Fergus rounded on him. "I'm not the King's—" Then he caught himself, as if he feared to speak to the gray-cloaked wizard.

Conor pushed past him and faced Myrddin. "I am Conor, as you have said. But how did you know it? You called me by name, before I had spoken it."

Myrddin chuckled softly, and once again Conor heard the hidden undercurrents of power in his voice. But the magician's words were gentle enough. "I could tell you that it is a wizard's business to know such things, and leave you to wonder how and what I do know. But I will not. How do I know your name, Conor? It's simple. For thirty leagues you've been asking after me, and telling all you meet exactly who you are."

Fergus couldn't help himself. "Aye, he's a blabberhead," he broke in sourly. "No doubt about that."

"And you, Fergus Ironhand," Myrddin continued smoothly. "Are there any who live in the world who haven't heard of you, of your loyalty, your bravery, your prowess in battle?"

Fergus paused, stared, then turned away again. But there was a flush of color on his cheeks. "Well, now," he muttered.

"At any rate, I need no sorcerous powers to know when two such mighty heroes approach my humble dwelling. I have known of your coming for days now. In fact, I expected to see you much sooner, but you did not come. After more waiting than should have been, I set out myself to look for you. And now I've found you. But too late, I fear. Too late!"

With that, Myrddin threw back his hood, revealing hair the color of tarnished silver that fell to his shoulders, a flowing beard of the same color, though scratched with streaks of smoky black, and the hooded, piercing eyes of an eagle . . . if an eagle's eyes should be the color of the skies through which it winged.

He raised his right hand and pointed across the river. "For you did not come alone," he said. "Catlin the warrior woman, and the apprentice mage Tullius also came with you, but they are not with you now. They are . . . over there!" He held for a moment, fingertip rigid, then let his arm fall. Shaking his head, he turned toward Conor. "Lad, lad. Why didn't you come to me first? I could have spared you much grief." His gaze settled on Conor's face, his eyes gleaming like snowshadows under a winter moon.

But it was Fergus who spoke next. "You know about Tully and Catlin, then? And how is that? There was no one rushing to carry word of their fate back across the water. At least, none that I saw."

Myrddin's eyebrows rose. "There is much of the Isle of Apples than no human eye can see," he said. "Some call it the Isle of Shadows, and rightly so. But that isn't your question, is it? You suspect me, don't you?"

"I didn't say that."

"You didn't have to. It's plain enough in your words, hide it as you will. Well. It is not my custom to explain myself, but I will tell you this: No spell of mine, nor even my hand, had anything to do with the fate of your friends. If you knew more than you do, you would know why that can be nothing but the truth."

Fergus, however, would not be mollified. "But I don't know more, do I? All I know is what I see. And I see you, the first living man who has approached us in many days. And you seem to know our trials well enough."

"Fergus . . ." Conor said, a tone of warning in his voice.

"No, lad. You're too trusting. And I don't trust this wizard . . . if wizard is what he is," he finished ominously.

Myrddin's eyes began to blaze with a cold blue fire that sent Conor leaping between the two men. Fergus's jaw jutted, even as Myrddin raised his staff.

"Hold!" Conor said. "Enough!" He turned to

Fergus and shoved him sharply backwards. "Stop it now. We already know how little we know. Spirits above, Fergus, you were ready to bury them! If Myrddin can help us, why not let him? For once in your life, *hold your tongue!*"

For a moment it looked as if Fergus might strike back, but then he unclenched his big fists and let his arms fall to his sides. He stepped back another pace, and when he spoke, his voice was surprisingly mild.

"You are like your father, Conor. You trust too much, and too easily. But I will not gainsay you. Do what you must." And with that, he walked several paces away and sat down cross-legged on the grass, his back to them.

"He is a great warrior, and all such have a fire inside them," Myrddin said. "I understand, and take no offense. He believes he has your good at heart."

Conor stared at Fergus's rigid shoulders, then sighed and turned back to the wizard. "Aye, he does, and no doubt of it. And there is much to what he says, Myrddin. I may be young, and as he says, my inclination may be to trust. But I'm not entirely stupid. So I must ask you. Tell me of yourself, and how you happen to be in this place at this time, and with so much knowledge of all that has happened to us." Conor paused, the corner of his lip suddenly quirking. "Even if you are not accustomed to explanations, I must have one. Or the two of us go no further."

Once again the quick, wintry gleam flashed out beneath those bushy gray eyebrows, but only for a moment. Then the wizard seemed to relax. "Very well," he said. "Let us go sit on the bank of the river, and I will tell you all you want to know. More, perhaps, than you desire."

"I will judge that for myself," Conor said.

"Yes," Myrddin replied, "that you will."

# FIVE

## THE CASTLE OF GLASS

—1—

Conor followed Myrddin to a grassy hump high on the bank above the river, but well downstream from where Fergus sat glowering. The wizard spread the skirts of his robe as he settled to the soft turf. Conor noticed that though Myrddin looked old, his movements were graceful and precise, as if the years had not touched him beyond the gray in his hair and the deep wrinkles at the corners his eyes.

Conor dropped down next to him, and for a moment they both sat in silence, staring at the rush of the water before them. Finally Conor lifted his gaze toward the Isle of Apples on the far shore.

"They both ate of the apples on that island," he said. "And now they are stone. But I ate that fruit as well, and I am still whole and unharmed."

Myrddin eyed him sideways. "I hear the secret question in your words, Conor. Fear not! The fate of your friends is not yours." He raised one hand and pointed at the distant shore. "That is Avallon, the long home of the Aes-Sidhe. It is not really there, not in the way you think of such things. The fact that you see it at all, let alone are able to cross the water, marks you as foredoomed. The Great Spirits who live there have circled you out, you and your rough-hewn accomplice." Myrddin glanced over at Fergus, who still sat facing away, seeming to ignore them. The wizard smiled faintly.

"Foredoomed," Conor said. "I don't like the sound of that."

"Call it fated, then. The High Ones have set a path beneath your feet, and you must follow it." Myrddin shrugged. "Or turn away, but then you contest their will, and that might work ill for all your hopes. Not to mention the plight of Tullius and Catlin, now caught in the stone dreams of the Sidhe."

The light beyond the river was a golden sheet that obscured vision. For a moment it looked impossibly dreamlike to Conor, and he found himself doubting that he'd ever crossed beyond the water. Or that he would ever find his way back.

"I am a warrior, Myrddin. How am I involved with such things? You speak of the doings of the Highest Spirits, those whom even the Druids fear to name aloud."

Myrddin nodded. "I do speak thus. For though I am not privy to the private deliberations of the mightiest, nor do I know their hidden aims and goals, they are not entirely strangers to me." He paused, gazing fixedly at the lighted land beyond the water. "Once that place was my home too," he said softly.

Conor felt his skin prickle. "Then . . . you are a god?"

Myrddin chuckled. "Say instead that when the gods frolic, their children may partake of their nature and powers."

"Still, I fear the blood of the Deathless runs in your veins."

"Aye, I am both older and younger than I look," Myrddin said. "Let that be your first lesson, Conor, not to judge things on their surfaces, or on appearances that may be masks as easily as truth."

"Now you sound like Fergus."

"Then your warrior is wise, in his own way," Myrddin agreed. "But come, lad. None of this has much to do with you, perhaps, though you have come seeking me. Now you've found me, and it is time to unburden yourself. Why have you come? What do you seek, here in the perilous world on the edge of dreams?"

Once again Conor felt that curious, prickly sensation of warning. But the wizard was right. Conor had been seeking him for weeks, and had risked— and lost—much to bring himself to this moment.

"There is a curse upon the Land," he said slowly. "The skies are bleak and cold, and no sun shines. The crops wither, and those planted new don't push their green stalks above the hard, barren ground. My people are starving, and evil things move among them. I came seeking you, whose reputation has become known far to the south, in lands you may not even have heard of. I came seeking your help."

A small breeze came up and ruffled Myrddin's hair. He sighed. "I know much, young Conor. Your lands are no mystery to me, though I don't go there as much as I once did, or"—his voice dropped mysteriously—"as much as I will once again, perhaps." He raised his eyebrows and stared questioningly at Conor. But Conor had no idea what was wanted, and only shook his head.

"What?"

Myrddin paused a beat, then shrugged. "No matter. Some know their fate beforehand, and some not. It makes no difference, and we will go on anyway. I know of the curse on the Land. What would you have of me, then?"

"A wizard's hand!" Conor said suddenly. "*Your* hand, Myrddin. If the curse is magic, then magic will cleanse it. That is what I seek of you. Will you help me?"

But Myrddin didn't reply at once, merely stared blankly out across the water, as if remembering something he'd nearly forgotten. "Ah," he said finally. "I was once as young as you, Conor."

Conor waited, not understanding, but when Myrddin said nothing else, Conor prodded him. "And so . . . ?"

"And so the worlds on both sides of the dream were simpler places then."

He seemed to expect Conor to understand this, but Conor felt himself floundering. The words of wizards were subtle, he knew that well enough. Galen had sometimes seemed to speak in nothing but riddles, and even the child Blas had been a puzzle more often than not.

But he had no time for subtlety. "Speak plainly, Myrddin. What you say is beyond me. Yet I need to know—can you help me? Will you?"

Myrddin hesitated the smallest of moments before answering. "Yes, Conor, I can help you. But first, you will have to help me."

He sighed. "Even when the world was young, the balance had to be kept. Though the world has changed, that has not. Tit for tat, young warrior. And then I, Myrddin, will raise the curse from your Land. I promise it!"

Conor didn't lift his head. This was what he'd sought. So why did he feel that not only he, but the Land itself, were in even greater danger than before?

Fergus was right. The meanest warrior's sword was simpler and more trustworthy than the most powerful of wizard's wands.

Yet with Tully and Catlin entombed within their own stony skins, he knew he had no better choice. Only now, though, did he begin to suspect that such had been the case all along. Rats and dogs! Why couldn't life be *simple?*

"Tell me what I must do," he said.

—2—

They walked slowly along a grassy ridge, a low backbone of earth that bisected, in a natural causeway, the lands that sloped gently away to either side. Here were fields dotted with bright flowers, red, golden, and purple, over which clouds of bees hummed ceaselessly. A soft breeze made silent, rippling paths across the blossoms, its faint whisper vying with the distant liquid hiss of the river against its banks.

Up ahead a strange silver fog began to grow, at first a mere hand's-width of fume obscuring their path, but as they came closer, billowing up into a broad, high curtain of mist.

"What is that?" Conor asked. He could hear Fergus clumping along behind, muttering to himself.

"That? Poor as it is, there is my home, at least my home in this world," Myrddin said.

They approached the nearest fringe of this mysterious silver haze, and a moment later, passed on through. Immediately the way became nebulous and hidden. Conor fancied he could hear voices, some far, some near, crying out wordlessly, but he could see nothing but a swirling mist, though shot with a thin, mercurial light that seemed to come from everywhere and nowhere.

He paused, turned, and looked over his shoulder. "Wait! Where is Fergus?"

Myrddin had hooded himself again. In the secrecy of his gray cloak he blended with the mist so completely that he was almost invisible, though Conor did see a flash or two of his ice-glinted eyes.

"He is coming," Myrddin said. "Close enough behind. Come, let us go on."

"No! We will wait." Conor planted his feet, his face turned back down the path, but he saw nothing. "Fergus!" he cried suddenly. "Where are you?"

After a moment he heard an answering shout, though it sounded thin, attenuated, far away. He whirled on the wizard.

"What have you done? He was right behind us just a moment ago. If this is some sorcerous trickery, stop it. I won't go on without him!"

All Conor could see of the magician now was the dark opening in the hood that cloaked his skull.

"It's not trickery, Conor. Here he is now, just a little slow-footed, but quite unharmed, I assure you."

Indeed, Fergus's large shape now appeared, moving up the path behind them. He had his hands to his mouth, and was shouting Conor's name.

"Here I am, Fergus!"

"Oh. Yes. For a moment there . . ." Fergus glared at the magician. "Nothing but this cursed fog. I thought you were gone."

"Well, I'm not. Stay close this time."

Fergus snorted. "Hang on to your apron strings, boy, is that it?"

"Hang on to your temper, more like," Conor muttered, turning away.

The fog began to lose its silvery gray shadows and show sudden darting flashes of color. Conor moved up abreast of Myrddin, feeling the breath of a fresh wind blowing toward him, heavy with the perfume of hidden herbs. He smelled cardamom and sage, wild parsley and sweet pea, even a deep hint of lily. The scattered gleams grew brighter, slipping and flowing, until the very air seemed one vast dance of color.

"What is it?" Conor asked, his voice rough with awe.

"Some might call it a sorcerer's trick," Myrddin replied. "But it is not. These are but the memory of something older and far greater; the Veils of the Morning, that the *Tuatha da Daanan* wore like great cloaks when they rose out of the Uttermost West and brought the light of the first dawn onto the lands of men."

Then, as if his words were a signal, the vast, shifting curtains of color split apart to reveal a long greensward that rolled in soft emerald waves up to the crystal doors of the Castle of Glass.

—3—

Conor stopped dead, his jaw dropping nearly to his chest. Behind him Fergus, as stunned as a steer before slaughter, stumbled into him. Before them a forest of towers, each one a jeweled prism of countless colors, scratched topless claws against a sapphire sky. The light here seemed ever from the west, and so shone through the ways and passages and walls before them, and touched the battlements with a beauty beyond mortal ken.

Myrddin had stopped, and turned, and now regarded the two of them with an expression both quizzical and sardonic. "This is the Castle Glass, my home and exile in the world beyond the dreams of the Sidhe."

Still, neither Conor nor Fergus moved, frozen by the spectacle rearing before them. Castle Glass was nothing like any home they had ever seen—this vast forge, armory, puzzle work, fountain of light, an avalanche that both stimulated and numbed at the same time.

"You live here?" Conor finally managed.

Myrddin pushed back his hood a final time, exposing his gray locks, which in the rainbow pigments of that blazing edifice now took on the hues of silver melting in a bonfire. His eyes gleamed brightly as he laughed aloud.

"Oh, yes, for many years. More than I care to think about. Why? Do you think it grand? No doubt you do."

Conor's gaze crept from the castle to its chatelain, and back again. "You must be very great," he said softly.

Something flickered in Myrddin's gaze, but he only shrugged and replied, "Maybe once. And maybe once again, but only the years will know that tale. Come, you've gawked enough. We have much to speak of. Let us go."

Conor nodded, the spell finally broken. He took a step on the path, and then another. Fergus shook himself, and followed. As he came close, Conor spoke without turning. "What do you think of magic now, Fergus?"

Fergus's voice was soft with wonder. "If that magic be dark, then we are doomed. But if not . . ."

"I wonder what Longinus would think of it," Conor said.

"Speak not that name!" Myrddin said harshly. "It is stained with a great curse, and the curse is not yet unraveled to its final end. Yet it touches on you, as I will explain. When we are safely inside. Come."

With that, Myrddin strode forward until he approached the vast, faceted doors of the castle itself. Here he halted and raised his staff. Conor heard no words, but felt a sudden rush of heat against his face. In utter silence, smooth as oil slickering across still water, the gates split, and rolled open, and they passed on through.

—4—

The rooms beyond the high gates of Castle Glass were yet another surprise. From the outside, the castle was like a pile of fantastic children's blocks, though clear as polished jewels. Inside, however, were walls of polished stone, as opaque as any other stones, and the only transparencies were the great windows cut into those finely fitted walls. It took Conor several minutes to note yet another strange charm of the place: No matter what direction the windows faced, they all gave out on a vista to the west, of Avallon, basking golden beneath a noon-high sun.

Myrddin led them up broad stairs covered with thickly woven carpets, beneath walls hung with tapestries that showed monsters and heroes, and the High Spirits watching all with grave, remote eyes.

Conor slowed as he passed one such scene, for on it a mighty warrior struggled against a great, snarling dog. "Who is that?" he asked.

Myrddin glanced at it and offered a faint, knowing smile. "In the deeps of time, Cuchulann, blessed of the Sidhe, tore the smith's hound limb from limb, and thus first proved worthy of the great quests that would be set before him. But come, Conor, did you need ask? Surely you know the old tales as well as I? At least these old tales . . ."

Conor glanced at him, then nodded. He wasn't quite sure if the wizard was answering him or mocking him. Perhaps both. Once again he felt a faint intimation of danger, and warned himself to be on guard against trickery. Or worse.

They saw no others, not warriors, or servants, or slaves, in their quick passage upward. Conor could hear Fergus grumbling under his breath as he brought up the rear, and hid his own smile behind his hand. No doubt there was more than enough magic about to keep the old thunderer thoroughly upset.

Finally they reached the top of a mighty staircase that gave onto a wide balcony overlooking a room large enough to hold a small village. Myrddin turned to the right, and opened a heavy wooden door. He stepped aside and motioned them through, bowing with what Conor suspected was more than a bit of mockery as he pointed the way.

"I have prepared a meal for you," Myrddin

said as they went in. He gestured toward a thickly carved oak table against the far wall, laden with platters of steaming meat, tankards of frosty ale, and bowls of fruit and rich, yellow cheese.

Conor felt his mouth begin to water at the sight of such a feast. He sniffed, and grinned as the savory odors filled his nose.

"Wait, lad," Fergus grunted as Conor started forward. "I wouldn't, if I were you."

Myrddin, ignoring the repast, had wandered toward a high window and now stood, his elbow on the stone sill, gazing pensively out toward the west. "There's nothing magical about it, Fergus. It's all real, from my own herds and orchards. There are no spells on those viands, and even you may eat without fear."

Fergus grunted again, but his beaked nose was twitching now as he moved reluctantly toward the table. Conor quickly filled a polished wooden trencher, and using a golden knife began to lift steaming, gravy-sodden chunks of beef toward his mouth.

"Don't eat if you don't care to, Fergus," he said. "More for me that way."

Fergus aimed a halfhearted glare in his direction, but after another moment of hesitation, he too began to load a trencher. He paused after his first bite, shoulders hunched, and looked up at the ceiling as if he expected to be struck by lightning. But nothing happened except that Myrddin chuckled softly and said, "Even the apples are safe, Fergus. Go on, eat. It may be your last chance for a time."

Conor lowered the haunch on which he was gnawing, his expression suddenly growing serious. "Yes, we must speak of that. You tell me I must help you before you will help me . . ."

Myrddin didn't turn, but continued to stare out the window. His voice, when he replied, was distant, as if his thoughts were elsewhere. "Not before I *will* help you, Conor, but before I *can* help you."

Conor walked toward him, until they stood shoulder to shoulder. "I don't understand."

"Of course not. How could you? You think the curse a small thing, some bit of wizardry perhaps ordered up by Diana, the Roman woman who would be a queen. But it is not. The roots of this curse are high and deep, deeper than you imagine, higher than you know. The Spirits themselves have woven this skein, for what purpose I do not know."

"The Sidhe? They cast this curse?"

"I did not say that! As I told you, I don't purport to know the thoughts of the High Ones. But what I can tell you is this. You, Conor, are the cause of the curse. You brought it on your own people by your own deed, and if I am to lift it, it will come only after you have done what it necessary to undo what you have already done."

"The curse is my fault?" Suddenly the food he'd been eating sat in Conor's belly as heavy as a sack of lead sinkers. He put down his plate. "But how can that be? I'm no magician."

"Yet you meddle in the affairs of wizards!" Myrddin shook his head. "You even play with forces a wizard might fear to encompass. And so you bring down your own doom not only on yourself, but your people also."

"What are you *talking* about? I've done no meddling."

Myrddin turned and fixed his blue gaze, cold as the rime frozen on a winter freshet, on his face. "Oh? What about Longinus? What about the Spear?"

"The . . . Spear?"

"Come, Conor, don't play the fool with me. The Spear of Destiny. You flung it into the sky, from whence it did not return. You had your reasons, and I know them as well as you do. But you gave no thought to other consequences beyond your own. Yes, you saved yourself, but at the cost of disturbing another balance. The Spear and Longinus, Longinus and the Spear. The two of them, wound and bound together through endless time, their mutual destiny not yet consummated. But you gave no thought to that, did you? And now the Spear waits beyond the world, and in the place it should have been now lies a curse. Your curse, Conor."

"But I . . . I . . ."

"That is plain garbage, wizard!" Fergus broke in, his heels slamming hard on the stone flags as he stomped toward them. "The Spear was evil, and doing evil. Conor did the right thing to get rid of it!"

"Did he, fearless warrior? Don't let your fear of magic blind you! You know nothing of what you speak, nor does he."

"And I suppose you do?" Fergus sneered.

Myrddin turned to face him, his right hand tightening on his staff. "You overstep yourself. I will tolerate your ignorance, but not your disrespect. Surely not in my own house."

"Oh? And what do you propose to do about it?"

Conor started to move between them, but Myrddin raised his staff. "Hold, young prince! This one needs a lesson. Just as I wouldn't presume to teach him swordplay, he will learn not to instruct a wizard about magic!"

With that he twirled the tip of his staff in a small circle as he spread the fingers of his left hand wide and pointed them at Fergus.

Bright sparks bloomed and fizzed at his fingertips. A single beam of pale blue light leaped forth, bathing Fergus in its radiance. Fergus froze in midstride, his mouth gaping like that of a stunned fish. Then, in a flash, he flew across the room and fetched up against the wall, halfway between floor and ceiling, pinned by invisible bonds like a fly caught on a heap of dung.

Myrddin's blue eyes glittered dangerously. "It is only because I am a reasonable sort that you are on that wall instead of through it, Fergus. And so you learn that not all power comes from naked steel. Say it!"

Fergus's jaw worked as if he were cracking stones with his teeth. Sweat sprang out on his brow. But he could not move.

"Say it," Myrddin said again, but more softly.

"I . . . yield . . ." Fergus finally gasped. Myrddin nodded, and set down his staff again. Fergus came unstuck from the stone and fell in a heap on the floor with a sound like a bag of wheat dropped from a tree.

"Fergus!" Conor cried, rushing over to him. He bent over and helped the older man to his feet. Fergus stood with a dazed look on his face, rubbing a freshly purpled knot on his bony noggin.

"You could have hurt him!" Conor said.

"Not by dropping him on his thick skull," Myrddin replied. He gestured again with his staff, and Conor flinched. "Anyway, you came seeking me, not the other way round. And if your man will not learn common courtesy, then I will teach it to him. Anyway, enough! If you wish to have my help, then we will go on. If not, then you will go. Say now, boy, because I have other things on my mind than your petty troubles."

Fergus made a choking sound and lurched forward, but Conor swung round and caught him in a hug. "Will you *stop* it, you old bear?"

Fergus strained against him, then relaxed suddenly. "I don't like this, and I don't like him."

Conor pushed him back. "I hadn't noticed. So let's agree you've made your point. And if you try to make it further, I'll be peeling you off the wall again."

Fergus turned away. "Maybe I'll have a bit more of that grub over there."

"Good idea," Conor said. "Anything to keep your mouth busy with other than words."

But Fergus ignored this, and with great dignity marched back toward the banquet, carefully ignoring Myrddin's hawk-eyed stare.

Conor watched Fergus for a moment, then returned to the wizard. "I wish he wasn't that way sometimes, but he is," he said softly. "Now tell me what I must do. You say the Spear of Longinus is the cause? I had thought the world a better place with the Spear out of it, but you say otherwise. So is that my quest? To find the Spear and return it to its rightful place?"

Myrddin's eyes narrowed in thought. After a moment he shook his head and sighed. "It may well be, Conor. I cannot say for certain. You see, the Spear is one of the Four."

"The Four?"

"The Four Great Talismans. The Spear, the Cauldron, the Sword, and the Stone. These were the gifts the Sidhe brought out of the dawn to the world of men, when the First Age was young, and the light new on the world."

Conor stared at him in puzzlement. "I didn't know of these four gifts, or Talismans. Are they in the old stories?"

"Some of the old stories. The tales shift, and sometimes the Talismans wear disguises. But in truth they are these: the Spear of Lugh, the Sword of Nuadu, the Stone of Fal, and the Cauldron of Dagdha. They are called by many names, however— for instance, you know Lugh's Spear as Longinus's Spear of Destiny, and think it a part of that sorcerer's curse. But it is far older than his curse, and its origin begins long before the ruin of the god that ensnared one Roman centurion."

Conor strained to get his thoughts around all this, for it was completely new to him. And it was far deeper and more perilous than anything he'd suspected before.

"Are you saying, then, that the disappearance of the Spear, when I cast it into the sky, was a graver matter than simply the evil it seemed to do?"

"Indeed, Conor, it was. Not all the world revolves about you, Longinus, the Alliance, and the Land. Although for you those must naturally be the most important things, for they are your fate."

At first Conor didn't realize the import of what the wizard had just told him. Only after a moment's thought did it sink in, and he felt his blood cool with a chill of terror. "You mean I am fated? That the Spirits of the West know my name?"

"But how could you doubt it, Conor? Think! Look at your own past. One doom after another, blood and death, fate and life. You were born to be a hero, whether you would or not."

"But I don't want to be."

Myrddin shrugged. "All of us are doomed in one way or another. You are. I am. Even that lout over by the table."

"Hey!" Fergus said.

Myrddin ignored him. "But only a few of us receive the personal regard of the High Ones. It can be a taste of eternal glory, Conor, the most perilous and awesome fate a mortal can endure. Or it can be a fall such as human thoughts cannot begin to conceive. And all of it rests on our own shoulders." He smiled faintly. "If we can bear it."

"I cannot!" Conor cried out.

"You have so far. Or you would not be here. And"—Myrddin raised his head and stared appraisingly at the younger man—"I think you will continue."

"This is . . ."

"No matter at all. Not to us, not now, not with what lies before you. And before me. I said you must help me if I am to help you. And so you must. Will you accept the quest, or no? Speak quickly, for there isn't much time."

Conor's thoughts were whirling as if a great storm raged behind his eyes. Fate and doom! The eyes of the gods! It was all a far cry from what he thought he knew of himself. How had he gotten into this snare? Was Myrddin telling the truth, or was this part of some larger trick he couldn't yet grasp?

He licked his lips. "I will accept it, if you will tell me what it is."

"The Cauldron of Dagdha, Conor. One of the Four. In this time and place you know it differently. In the tales of the Land it is the Bowl of Plenteous Cure. You must find it, and bring it to me. Only then can I use the power of it to lift the curse from the Land—and not incidentally, restore your friends to life!"

"And where can I find this thing?"

"Where else, Conor? Where did you think? It lies hidden on the Isle of Apples, where you must return. Seek it on Avallon, boy, long home of the gods, on the other side of the Dream. Seek it in the hands of Bran the Sleeping Lord, in his perilous Castle of Four Horns. There is where you will find your doom, to live or die as the fates allow. What say you now, Conor Derek's Son?"

Conor stared long out the window at the shining land beyond. Finally he turned and looked into Myrddin's glimmering blue eyes.

"I don't think I am what you say I am," he said. "But if I can do this thing, I will."

"That is good, then," Myrddin said.

# Six

## The Journey Begins

— 1 —

It was dawn in the east, a thin gray line surmounted by darkness and a fading spray of stars, though eternal light still blazed to the west beyond the enchanted river. Conor, Fergus, and Myrddin the Mage came down from Castle Glass and paused for a moment on the grassy bank.

Myrddin had fitted them with fine new cloaks, whose colors were hard to discern, for they shifted with every change of the light, now brown, now grassy green, now blue as still pools.

"Wear them always," Myrddin warned, "for they will protect you in time of need, even from eyes far sharper than mortal men have."

Fergus fingered the soft, fine fabric of his cloak and grunted. "If they keep away the cold and repel the rain, I'll be happy enough."

Myrddin cocked one bushy gray eyebrow at

him. "It would be well if weather was all you had to fear, Fergus, but you know better. Your quest, and that of your master, is more perilous than that. The Horned Keep, where Bran lies in guarded sleep, is ringed with many terrors. You will have your own time of testing, just as Conor, and then you will be glad to have my poor gifts."

"Prophecy," Fergus muttered. "Dark prophecy. I don't like it." His chin jutted as he aimed his own gaze at the magician. "And you can stick me to a wall like a fly if you want, but I don't like you, either."

Myrddin, who had unhooded himself and left his hair to flow freely to his shoulders, threw back his head and laughed. "Well, I can't say as you're my most favored guest either, oh, crusty warrior. I've had better, and surely many whose manner was smoother. But I think you have a stout heart and are true to Conor and his line, so I let it pass."

Fergus, unsure whether he was being complimented or insulted, and suspecting a little of both, snorted and began to pull at the ends of his mustache as he turned away.

"And you, Conor," Myrddin said, "remember what I have told you."

Conor nodded, and began to speak softly.

*In the bright morning*
*Of dawn never ending*
*Take the bowl ever spending*
*From the horns never bending . . .*

Myrddin nodded. "I don't know what you will face before you reach the tomb and keep of the

Sleeping One. I am no longer a part of the endless dance, for that is my own wound and curse. But the High Ones only concern themselves with mortals by whim or chance, for their interests go to the long silver dark before the World, and men are but one page of their unfolding tales. Keep it in mind, Conor. You go not to a mortal place, and you will not always be welcome. So be wary!"

Conor nodded. "I will try. And we will go armed. Our weapons still lie, I hope, on the other bank, where we left them next to our friends. The sword of my father, and Fergus's great blade, and the Gae Bolga that I found."

Myrddin sighed and squinted at the moving waters. "The Gae Bolga. I don't understand that. I believe it came to your hand for a reason, though I don't know what the reason is. Keep it close and always ready, Conor. It may save you many times in your quest—though how, I cannot say."

Conor nodded. "I will."

Myrddin spread his hands wide as he faced the river. The first rays of dawn struck his high forehead and changed the look of his face, so that for a moment Conor saw his true lineage revealed, and through his mask of sadness the memory of great joy. And he knew that the blood of the Deathless did run in Myrddin's veins, and that his powers, though hidden, were great.

Myrddin sensed his regard, and nodded. "I cannot go there, Conor, and you cannot know the sadness of that. Mayhaps one day I shall be allowed to return to my rightful place, but much lies before me, and many long years of toil and duty. I bear my curse, and so do you. But at least to you is given a chance to amend your deeds and find release and joy. For me . . . well . . ."

He shrugged. "If I could truly envy a mortal, then I envy you. Good speed, and all the luck you will need. Now go. And make all haste to return to me with what you seek and I need."

Conor took Myrddin's right hand in his own and held it, feeling the great strength of the wizard's grip. "I wish you were coming with us. This task may be beyond my strength."

"If so, then the worse for both of us. But I do not believe it so—the weavings of the *Tuatha da Daanan* are shifty and hard to decipher. Yet you were sent to me for a reason, and I see your doom and fate."

Suddenly he smiled, and Conor felt an answering surge of hope and joy. "But all is not doom and fate, Conor, and it is given to mortal men to have some hand in the weaving of their own. You have choice and luck. May both be good for you. And now I say again, go. It is time, and dawn is as good a starting point as any."

With that, Myrddin thrust out his right hand and pointed to the great green fire of the Morning Star, which was set in place at the beginning of the heavens, before even the lamps of moon and sun.

"May the light of the Star guide your feet and your heart, Conor."

Conor lifted up his gaze to the emerald flame, and when he looked back down, Myrddin was gone. Nothing remained of him but the imprint of two shod feet, slowly springing back from the green grass.

Conor had not seen him go, and Fergus, who had shown the both of them his disapproving back, had not, either.

"He's gone, Fergus. You can quit pouting now. He's gone, and it's time we were gone as well."

Fergus turned and stared at the place the wizard had been, and his expression lowered even further. "That one speaks fine words, Conor, but I wager his aims have little or naught to do with us, except as we can help him with his own desires. I would not trust him!"

"Yet what other choice do we have, Fergus? Have you a better?"

Fergus said nothing.

"I didn't think so. And since you don't, are you coming or staying?"

"I will go with you, Conor, because I am pledged to you, and none will ever say that Fergus broke pledge with any man, let alone the captain of his people. But my heart is uneasy."

Conor moved to him and took him around the chest and hugged him. "Good old Fergus. What would I do without you?"

"Worse than you have," Fergus said sourly.

But he said no more, and after a moment they slipped into the water beneath the dwindling light of the Mornstar, and presently disappeared beyond the silver-tipped waters, like dreams fading before the light of day.

—2—

They came up from the river into the Land of the Dream dripping and blowing, and paused for a moment at the verge to dry themselves. Conor looked back the way they had come, and though he knew dawn was now burning brightly there, he saw only the dim and the gray, as if the light of mortal worlds would always be less than the fire of the Undying Lands.

"What are you looking at?" Fergus said. "That damned wizard isn't back, is he?"

"No, he's gone."

"Good. That was half the reason I wanted to return across the river—that he couldn't follow. Or at least he said he couldn't. Not that I'm sure you can believe anything he says."

"Fergus, why don't you trust him?"

"Because it's magic, Conor. I'm a warrior. I trust things I can see and touch. Things that don't change on some whim I cannot understand. Give me solid ground under my feet, and a pot of beer in my hand, and my sword and something to strike with it, and I'm happy. We are mortals, Conor. Magic comes from outside our world, and has no place in it. Or so it seems to me."

Conor nodded, because he truly did understand. It wasn't that Fergus was afraid, as much as he was offended. Magic broke the rules. And it did so in sometimes horrifying ways. If magic held sway, then mortals could count on nothing, and nothing was sure. But then, mortal life wasn't sure either, was it? A man could go to meet his true love, and return to find his family in red ruin, slaughtered in the midst of joy. Or he could hold his love in his arms, her blood running down his sleeve from wounds suffered at the blade of her own father. All things were chance. Nothing was certain.

"You have come with me," Conor said softly. "That is enough."

"It will have to be, won't it?" Fergus replied. Then he smiled suddenly and clapped Conor on the back, hard enough to nearly send him sprawling. "Besides," he roared, "without me, bratling, who would keep you out of trouble?"

"Not you, surely," Conor replied, laughing. "Trouble is your middle name."

But Fergus turned somber. "My kind of trouble may give you a hangover or, at worst, threaten your life in some kind of brawl. But your soul is safe, Conor."

"And it isn't here?"

Fergus shivered. "Nothing is safe here, Conor. Nothing at all."

Conor picked his cloak up from the grass, noticing how its colors had shifted until it was nearly invisible against the sun-dappled sward. He flung it around his shoulders and secured it with a silver clasp. "We will have to go on anyway."

Fergus donned his own cloak. "Yes. But I fear I may not return across the water from this place."

Conor made no reply, for even as reassuring words sprang to his lips, he realized they were lies. He didn't know. What Fergus said might well be true.

In the end he turned away from the river and said, "Whatever comes, it's time to begin now."

Fergus nodded, and followed him across the meadow, where fat bees danced above fresh-blooming flowers, beneath a sun that never died. And despite all foreboding, for a moment hope swelled in both their hearts. For this was Avallon; and where the Aes-Sidhe walked, nothing could ever be truly without hope.

—3—

They had come up to the Apple Isle a fair trek downstream from where they had left Tully and Catlin and their gear. Conor reckoned that a half hour of steady walking had passed, through slow-rising swales of grass, before Fergus, striding out ahead, stopped and called back, "Here they are!"

He came up and found Fergus stooping next to Catlin's still form, one big hand resting on her forehead. Fergus looked up at him, his anguish plain on his face, and said, "Poor lassie. Nothing's changed. Nor with Tully, either. They are stones, cool and dead."

"Not dead!" Conor said. "Only sleeping."

But Fergus shook his head. "If they are sleeping, then the rocks of the Land we know, which have not moved in the time of our fathers, and their fathers, and all before them, are also sleeping."

"The Druids can make even the stones dance," Conor replied.

"Yes." Fergus spat. "With magic."

Conor left him there, sunk in his dark thoughts, and went over to the small cache they had left. Everything seemed untouched. He found his father's sword and strapped it on. The Gae Bolga, which he had polished, gleamed with the dull silvery glow of well-tended steel. He picked it up and hefted it. Though it was a strange weapon, he judged it deadly enough.

There also were Tully's knives and Catlin's bow and quiver. He considered. He had no idea how long their journey would be, and had no wish to be weighted down beneath a whole armory of weapons. But while he considered, he looked beyond the small pile of their things and saw something new: there, on the grass, nearly invisible, a pair of packs seemingly made of the same material as their cloaks. So perfectly did they blend in to the background, they'd escaped his initial notice.

"What's this?" he murmured.

Fergus heard him and stood, his long, craggy features still mournful, but wariness quickening in his eyes. "What's what?"

"Over here," Conor said. He went to the packs and opened the nearest. "Well. This is strange."

Fergus found his own great blade and strapped it across his back. Then, feeling suitably girded at last, he joined Conor. "Where did those come from?"

"I don't know. I judge it must be Myrddin's doing. The material is the same as our cloaks. And look. They are full of food. Dried apples, and salted meat, and even a jug or two of wine."

"Wizard's food."

"True enough, but you've eaten of it, and nothing evil happened. He must have thought of you, and your aversion to magic apples, and sent this to keep you happy and fat."

"Sent it? How so? He said he couldn't cross the water."

Conor felt a small stab of uneasiness. It was true. But if the wizard's power stopped at the riverbank, how had these come here?

"I don't know. If these are gift horses, Fergus, you can look at their teeth all you wish, but in the end, I judge we'll eat these steeds anyway."

"More weight to carry," Fergus grumped. But he knelt down. "Help me with it, lad. I'll take the bigger one."

Conor hoisted the larger of the two packs, and helped Fergus secure the straps across his shoulders. "Careful of my sword, boy. Make sure nothing tangles the hilts."

"Of course, old bear. And you do the same for me."

Fergus did so, and after a time everything was ready. Conor returned to his two companions, imprisoned within the tombs of their bodies, knelt, and kissed both Catlin and Tully on the forehead.

"I will come back and release you, or I will die in the trying," he whispered.

But they did not answer, and their flesh was cold and hard beneath his lips. After another moment he rose, and turned his back to them beside the river.

"Off we go," he said, and though his words

were hard to understand, so thick was his voice, Fergus nodded.

"You lead, and I will follow, and watch our backs," he said.

"Yes. And keep your arm strong and ready."

"My arm is strong," Fergus replied. "But whether it is strong enough, I do not know."

"Time will tell," Conor said. They set off.

The land through which they traveled was richer and softer than anything they'd ever seen, a place where the grass rubbed against their knees as comfortably as a cat, where stands of oaks and junipers reared like crowds of kings, their leafy crowns scratching the blue sky, their limbs crowded with small creatures that chattered and leaped, chirped and flew.

They walked through gilded orchards where the trees stooped low with a bounty of apples and pears and peaches, or other, strange fruits, yellow, orange, and green, that neither of them knew. In these fruited bowers pollen hung so heavy in the air that they strode through a golden haze, where the sunlight seemed to ripple and dance. Perfumes hung about them so that even when they left those places, the scent still wafted about them in tangible memory.

On and on they went, following the directions that Myrddin had given them: "The sun will not move, but even at high noon it casts some small shadow. Keep your shadow before you always, until you see the Mountains of Guard in the distance. Make for the highest of these, snow-crowned Ilmarin, the tall Watchtower, for on his tree-guarded knees rests what you seek."

Once again, because the sun did not set, they lost track of time, and began to keep the time of their own bodies. They slept when they were tired, and ate when they were hungry. Conor was the first to notice that whatever they took from their packs was replenished and made whole when they opened the sacks again.

"More magic," Fergus said sourly. But he ate anyway, because he would touch no fruit that grew there nor raise his sword against any of the animals that crossed their path. They saw many deer, all of them like the first doe, calm and fearless, who approached and eyed them with gazes of amber and gold. Rabbits leaped about, and smaller things scurried in the grasses; and once, far away, they saw on a sloping hillside sheep so large they seemed like horses, except fat and woolly white.

But they saw no horses or cattle, and no living being appeared in their way. The land was unspoiled, fresh and new, and without change. At times Conor felt as if he no longer walked, but that the world itself rolled slowly away beneath his feet.

Judging as well as they could, they reckoned that three days had passed before the jagged teeth of the Mountains of Guard thrust above the far horizon; and though the sun still blazed above them, it seemed that a band of darkness, sprinkled with hard, clear stars, was tangled in their stony grasp.

"Perhaps not all of the Blessed Isle lies beneath the noonday sun," Fergus said. "There is night in those hills, or I'm a blind man."

Conor grinned at him. "At your age, I wouldn't doubt it. But I see the darkness too. I wonder what it means. Myrddin didn't speak of it."

"I suspect there is much that wizard didn't say. Perhaps wisely—silent mouth doesn't betray secret heart."

But Conor ignored this, and stood with one hand over his eyes, peering intently at the vast wall of snow-topped stone far ahead.

"I think . . . Fergus, do you see it? A bit to the right of center, about halfway down the tallest peak? That gleam of red and gold, like a slow fire burning?"

"I see something," Fergus said doubtfully. "But your eyes are better."

"Well, then, at least Myrddin told no lie about this. It's where he said it should be. That is the glint of the Horned Castle."

"We'll know when we get there, won't we? But it's still very far away."

"It is," Conor agreed. "Are you tired yet? Shall we rest now, give your ancient bones time to recover before we go on?"

Fergus grunted as he shifted his pack. "Laugh if you will, Conor, but I see my doom there in the distance. I will carry my ancient bones into that fire, but whether they will carry me back out again, I can't say. But I fear the worst."

Conor turned back to him and put his hands on Fergus's wide shoulders. "I'm sorry. I tried to make a joke to lighten your mood—and mine too. Can you forgive me, old friend?"

Fergus stared at him, then nodded shortly.

"I am afraid," Conor said simply. "I fear for you, and for Tully and Catlin, and for the Land we left behind, poisoned by a curse. And I fear for myself. I shouldn't make jokes, but I do, because I can't think of anything else to lighten the darkness that presses on me. I can only say this, Fergus: Without you, I would still try to go on, but it would be hard. I wish you were in no danger, but I am glad to have you with me."

Fergus reached up and took Conor's hands in his own strong grip. "Sometimes I mistake you, lad. I forget who you are, and whom you came from. Joke if you will—and so will I, if I can think of any. The magic all around us scares me, so that sometimes I feel like an unblooded boy, ready to pee his britches at the first sign of danger."

He offered a snaggled grin. "But I'm no boy, as you delight in pointing out. Neither are you, and we will go on to whatever waits for us."

His grin grew wider. "Though if *you* feel a sudden need to pee, sing out. I might want to walk upwind of you."

Conor's lips twitched once, then again, and he burst out laughing. A moment later both men were rolling on the ground, pummeling each other, roaring at the top of their lungs. And in that moment of release they sealed something between them, and saw their fate and accepted it. Their fear did not entirely pass away, but they were able to laugh at it; and so it diminished, and pulled them together rather than pushing them apart.

They turned toward the Watchtower with renewed vigor, and made good time for several hours. When they made camp the sun still blazed overhead, but the dark that wreathed the mountains had grown, and there were many stars.

Also, hazy in the distance, a thin tendril of gray smoke rose straight up.

—5—

"Look at that meadow of flowers," Fergus said, "and tell me what you see."

They had eaten and slept and awakened again into a high, clear noonday, and the thin snake of smoke still rose before them. Conor had clasped his cloak about his shoulders and was shrugging into his pack when Fergus spoke. He looked at the meadow and said, "I see flowers. Spring sage and summer thyme, and small white rose blossoms."

"You look, but you don't see. Think, lad."

After a moment, Conor said, "The blooms bend and sway before the breeze. As always."

"Yes. But does that smoke bend? If the wind can move a blossom, how then does smoke rise straight up into the air?"

Conor pulled his pack-straps tight. "I don't know. But this is Avallon, and there is much I don't know. Nor you. All we can do is go on. Whatever it is, it will be revealed in time."

"Yes," Fergus said, hitching his own pack onto his back. "But smoke that stands without moving before the wind, like a signpost or a beckoning finger, is a thing to mark. We will go carefully, Conor. Remember the hellhound at the smithy."

Conor reached over his left shoulder and drew his blade halfway out of its sheath. The sun struck it and sent back a rippling shower of light.

"Yes, I remember. But maybe it is only a shepherd's hut."

"As you say, this is Avallon. Here are the Sidhe. And even a shepherd may be something beyond our mortal ken."

"Then we will go on, and find out." Conor grinned. "Maybe it will be a pretty girl. That would not be beyond my ken, though maybe you are too old to appreciate—or remember—such things."

Fergus let out a barking laugh. "If it *is* a pretty girl, then we will see. Perhaps she'll have her wits about her, and good taste as well, and prefer a full-grown man, a mature man."

"Or a man with hair," Conor said.

Fergus chased him over a low rise, and they continued on.

—6—

All during their trek the broad land had been gradually sloping upward, as the low meadows, woods, and orchards slowly gave way to a high plateau of rolling yellow grass, spotted here and there with stands of dark green hazel-bushes heavily laden with nuts as big as fists, like emeralds scattered on a blanket of gold.

Now the Mountains of Guard filled a fifth of the sky ahead, and the darkness above them another third. And though the noon-high sun had not moved, they had, and now their shadows stretched out before them a full pace, when before they had puddled at their feet.

Fergus glanced back over his shoulder and said, "We are walking out from under the sun, Conor. In our own world such a thing could not be. But here it is. Maybe we will also walk off the end of the world, and fall into darkness."

"That is a mighty stone fence before us, Fergus, and what we seek lies on its knees, not its back."

Indeed, the tiny red spark on Ilmarin had grown brighter and clearer, and now glowed as a small crimson eye, though flickering every once in a while as if winking at them. Conor had been taking its measure as they grew closer, and it seemed to him the Horned Castle, if that is what it was, rested on some vast shelf or scarp, backed by climbing cliffs, and guarded from the front by more stone steps that only the Highest might mount, so high and sheer they were.

Now from these crags a steady wind had begun to blow, cooling their faces, sharper and cleaner than the rich breezes they had felt till now. Conor smelled pine, and fresh snow, and mountain springs rimed with crystal ice—and these winds were stronger. But the smoke before them didn't waver.

The plateau on which they marched began to lose its sameness as great chunks of black granite split the golden grass, as if vomited up from far below, the first outliers of the greater rocks ahead. They had been dodging around these solitary piles, although once they halted in the shelter of a high, dark mound and ate a meal, protected from the growing wind. They dined at the lip of a spring that sprang from living rock and fell into a small pool from which it flowed out and lost itself in the grass.

Fergus reached into the icy water and scooped up some of the stones there, and held them up to the light. "Look, Conor," he said softly, and turned his hand to let them dribble slowly back. They fell in a shower of red and blue and green, smoothly catching and holding the golden light.

"A rich spring this is," Fergus said, "to cup gems the size of hen's eggs."

"Maybe we should fill the crannies in our packs," Conor said. "Many mouths could eat from the proceeds of such stones, should we return to the Land at last."

But Fergus only arched his eyebrows. "Then you would steal from the treasures of the Aes-Sidhe, lad?"

Conor shook his head. "No, you're right. Nothing here is meant for mortal lands. I keep having to remind myself."

"See that you keep on doing so." Fergus wiped his wet hand on his thigh. "I wish it were over, and we were going home, or better, already there."

"I know," Conor replied. "Well, the mountains

are considerably closer now. Perhaps we are nearly halfway through."

"Climbing those high stairs to the red fire that gleams above won't be an easy thing. And even if we do, the wizard spoke not of the tasks we face at the top of those cliffs. Unless he spoke to you in secret."

"No, he said nothing. Just that what we seek in is the Horned Castle, and we must bring it. He thought perhaps this Gae Bolga might be of use, though."

Fergus eyed the three-pronged spear, which now gleamed like a mirror. All along their walk Conor had been polishing it with handfuls of fine sand, with a scrap of cloth, and with the oil of his own skin. And though there had been a film of red rust all over it, when that was rubbed away it was revealed that the edges of those blades had not dulled, nor had their points been blunted in any way.

"Yes, you ought to be able to stick something pretty good with that," Fergus said. "Though it's an outlandish weapon."

"In an outlandish place, maybe the best kind," Conor said, though he sounded a bit tired, and he leaned on the triple spear to hoist himself up from the lip of the spring. "We'll go on. I judge the smoke is only a few hours ahead. There is a scape of black rocks there, higher than what we've seen before. Perhaps we should just go around it. There may be a pretty girl tending her fire there, but to tell the truth, Fergus, I'd rather go on and find whatever awaits us on the mountains. There will be many pretty girls, perhaps, but our fate lies ahead, and maybe our doom."

"First wise thing I've heard out of you in days," Fergus said. "That Conor would leave well enough alone, and not go directly toward the first trouble he sees? Who would have thought it?"

So they set off again, and Conor pointed at a direction that would take them far to the right of the smoke and the stones. But after they'd marched for a while, somehow the smoke was back in front of them, unwavering, rising toward the line that marked the division between sunlight and stars.

They tried a different direction, but the result was the same. No matter which path they tried, all trails led to this hidden fire.

The sky overhead was half-golden with sunlight and half-sable with a blaze of stars when Fergus said, "It seems our fated path begins before the Mountains of Guard."

The rocks were nearly upon them, though the source of the smoke finger was still concealed behind their bony ramparts. And whatever direction they took, their feet still led them to it.

"Fate or no, it seems we have no choice," Conor said. "So let's get it over with."

He hefted the Gae Bolga, which flashed back both sun and starlight. Fergus showed his teeth, and with a single sweeping surge, flashed out his own sword.

The dark rocks rose out of the last of the grass like the prow of a great ship. They began to climb.

A sharp-beaked hoodie crow suddenly flapped

down from above. It swooped low over their heads and shrieked harshly three times before vanishing in a rustle of black wings.

"An evil omen," Fergus muttered.

Conor raised his Gae Bolga in the director of the crow's disappearance. "We shall see," he said.

# SEVEN

## ERIU'S COTTAGE

—1—

With the sharp cawing cry of the hoodie crow still ringing in their ears, Conor and Fergus crept to the top of the jumbled stones and halted there, crouched just beneath the rim.

"Let me catch my breath," Fergus said.

Conor squatted near him, his expression troubled. "Maybe we should wait a while before crossing over."

But Fergus shook his head. "Nay, lad, we've come this far. Something wants us here, so let's get it done with." Yet Conor heard how the older man's voice wavered slightly as he spoke. Fergus was afraid, and trying as best he could to hide it.

He slapped Fergus on the knee. "As you say, then. Are you ready?"

Fergus nodded. Conor grinned at him and stood. "First across is first done," he cried. Then, light-footed as a goat, he leaped up onto the topmost boulder, Fergus scrambling up a moment later. The two men stood, shading their eyes, and looked down.

The upthrust ridge on which they stood was now revealed as an incurving ring of stone, open toward the mountains, but cupping within its outstretched fingers a tiny, meadowed valley. A spring gurgled out from the foot of the rocks on which they perched, into a clear and sparkling stream that meandered through the center of the vale, past a thatch-roofed cottage. Behind the cottage was a low thatched barn, and next to it was a kraal made of peeled logs. In the kraal stood a single cow, dun-colored and placid.

The courtyard of the cottage was swept clean. A path of paving stones led from the front door to the edge of the stream, and next to the wooden door of the house, hanging atop a high pole, was a large iron bell.

From the chimney of the place the smoke rose straight up. For the first time the scent of it reached their nostrils. Conor sniffed. "Smells like . . . I don't know . . . fall. Everything of that season, roasting pigs, slow-charred oak logs . . . home."

His voice was sad. Fergus, whose own mind was suddenly filled with ancient memories, knew that Conor was thinking of things long gone, when his life had been simple and without pain. There was a healing balm in that smoke. Nevertheless, Fergus remained on guard. Healing it might be, but it was still magic.

"Looks like nobody's home," he said after a while.

Conor shook his head. "No, somebody's there. Can't you feel it?"

"Besides the cow? Better hope it's not another fine little doggie, like the last one . . ."

Conor hefted his Gae Bolga. "Well, at least this time we'll be on our guard. Shall we go down?"

Fergus cast one final, jaundiced glance at the scene below, but shrugged. "You first, with your pig-sticker. I'll come behind, and charm the pretty girls, if there are any."

That made Conor smile a little. They began to pick their way downward through the ancient, cracked boulders, until finally they reached the spring at the bottom. There they stopped, and Conor crouched down and put his hand into the water.

"Cold. Very good," he said after he'd filled his palm and drunk. "You try it."

Fergus shook his head. He was gazing off toward the cottage, now less than fifty paces distant. Still nothing stirred there, though the smell of the smoke was stronger.

"Maybe we just go up and ring that bell, eh?" he said.

"Now, that's a good idea," Conor said, and set off walking. Behind him, Fergus grimaced, but followed. He held his great sword in a two-handed grip, out and questing, ready for anything.

In the meadow that surrounded the tiny stedding, bright yellow butter-flowers peeped up at them, and white winter-pea blossoms, and here and there a patch of purple clover-balls. But there were no bees. Instead, swooping back and forth like fine curtains in the wind, clouds of orange butterflies. One such flapped past Fergus's nose and left him reeling with the dusty scent of cinnamon and cloves.

The pavement flags that ran between door and stream glinted with tiny bits of quartz that veined the darker stone. The stones looked as if they'd been scrubbed only a moment before. A preternatural quietness shrouded the stedd: No birds sang, no creatures crept, no voices called.

Even the cow watched them, silent and big-eyed, cud moving slowly, as they stood at the end of the path and peered up at the cottage. Two windows, curtained and dark, flanked the wooden door. The door was smooth and polished and glowed with the passage of long years, as if worn down beneath the touch of countless hands.

Conor watched for a moment, then shrugged, cupped his hands around his mouth, and shouted, "Halloo, the house!"

Fergus jumped. "So loud?"

"Might as well let them know they have guests."

"Keep an eye out for their watchdog," Fergus said nervously.

But there was no reply of any kind. Even the cow, after eyeing them blandly for another moment, finally turned and, tail switching, wandered away from them. It was so quiet the soft crunch of her hooves against the grass was sharp and distinct.

"Halloo, is anybody home?" Conor cried out again. But his call echoed quickly away and vanished into the renewed silence.

Conor glanced at Fergus. "Ring the door-bell, eh?"

"No, wait!"

But Conor left him there, shaking his head, and walked briskly up the path. He came to the door, then turned and struck the bell a blow with the blades of his Gae Bolga.

The sound that rang forth shocked them both. Instead of a single clang, peal after clarion peal rolled across the valley, stunning their ears with the sound. The cow wheeled around and set up a terrific mooing, and stamped her right forehoof on the turf three times.

So deafening was the cry of that bell that Conor dropped the Gae Bolga and clapped hands over both ears. And so he remained, face screwed up, when the door of the cottage finally swung open, and he saw her standing there.

"So," she said, "you've finally come back to me."

But Conor was struck dumb, because though her beauty was the greatest he'd ever seen, he'd never seen *her* before in his life.

—2—

"Well? Don't just stand there. Come inside." She peered past Conor's shoulder and sighed. "I see you've brought that lout, Nuadu, with you. He can come too—but first he must wipe his big, dusty feet!"

There was a soft buzzing between Conor's ears. He wasn't sure, but he thought it had something to do with her eyes—they were wide and green and cool, and reminded him of moss-covered pools, bottomless and still, hidden in dark forests. Her hair was a flame of black light, rippling and winding across her shoulders and down her back. Across her pert nose was a dusting of freckles, a dab of speckled color against the smooth cream of her cheeks.

"I . . . uh . . . his name isn't Nuadu. It's Fergus. And I . . . I mean my name . . . I'm Conor."

She tilted her head back and looked up at him, planting her hands on a bounty of curving hips as she did so. Conor tried not to stare at the sweetly mounded richness of her breasts as they peeped above the top of her simple blue shift. He tried, but he failed.

"Conor? And Fergus, you say? But what kind of joke is this? I know you well, and him too." A flicker of anger marred the skin above her nose, between her arching brows.

"No . . . no . . . you must be mistaken. I've never been here before. I've never seen you." Blushing, he half turned away, looking for Fergus, and whispering under his breath, "I'd remember it if I had."

"What? You'd remember?" But she stepped back a little, opening the way inside, and said, "Well, perhaps you've forgotten. Conor, is it? Very well, I'll call you Conor. And him Fergus, as soon as he wipes his feet."

Fergus had come forward, but he halted on the threshold, looked down, and shuffled his feet on the doorstone before entering.

"Yes, that's good," she said. "Fergus." The name seemed to amuse her.

"And what will you call me, Conor who forgets things? Have you forgotten my name as well as your own?"

"Ah . . . mistress, I'm sorry. Forgive me, but I don't know your name. I've never known it . . . though I would like to."

Once again her gaze flickered and flashed a moment before subsiding. "So you *have* forgotten me. How should I feel about that, do you think?"

Conor felt as if he were moving slowly through a pool of quick-mud, in danger of being sucked down at any moment. "I hope you will think forgivingly of me," he said. "Had I known you before this moment, I would have forgotten nothing, nor would I, even though I lived a thousand moons."

For some reason this seemed to puzzle her as well. "Even though you live . . ." She shook her head. "'Tis a strange game you play with me, Conor. But as I said, I will play it with you. Come in, sit down. I've a meal cooking. It's nearly done—you took long enough to get here. I'd almost think you'd forgotten the way."

"But I don't know the way, lady. At least, I didn't until I came here just now."

One more time her great eyes flashed at him, but this time she said nothing, merely turned and gestured toward a table already set with trenchers carved from living crystal, which refracted and reflected the blaze dancing in the tall fireplace beyond.

Conor shuffled past her, feeling gawky and

stupid, and wondering when the buzzing in his brain would stop. Fergus had already seated himself, and was staring at the utensils before him. He picked up a golden knife with a handle made of horn, a great ruby inset into the butt of the grip. "Fancy stuff," he said as Conor sat down across from him.

"What's your name?" Conor asked again, and this time she paused, then said, "You remember it, but it is Eriu."

"Thank you, Eriu," he said. "It's a beautiful name. Like the sigh of the wind."

She smiled at that. The sight sent another rumble of meaningless noise through Conor's thoughts. He shook his head as if to clear his ears, and began to look around the interior of the cottage.

It seemed far larger than it had looked from the outside. The room in which they sat towered into dimness and a roof-beam cloaked with shadows. Conor stared up, blinking. For an instant, he'd caught a flash of movement in that gloom.

The hearth where Eriu stirred a huge pot would have dwarfed Fergus and Conor together. They could have danced inside its glowing pit. Off to either side were finely carved fruitwood cabinets of great size and excellent proportion, and beyond that, a wide bed draped in fine sheetings and piled high with thick pillows and blankets.

Conor stared at the bed, his eyes widening and softening with surmise, then turned back to where Eriu was now dishing a savory stew into a broad, polished wooden bowl. Silver garnitures bound the wood, gleaming softly in the firelight.

"Can I help you with that?" Conor asked.

She shook her head, but smiled at him again, and he felt another wave of dizziness swirl through his poor, battered brain.

"It smells wonderful, doesn't it, laddie?" Fergus murmured.

Conor stared at him in surprise. The big warrior's features had gone soft and slack, his eyes dreamy as pools. A faint smile played on his lips, as if he were listening to some distant and wonderful music. He seemed totally at ease, all his fears soothed away.

For some reason, that made Conor feel uneasy. Fergus, who hated and feared all magic, was sprawled peacefully at table in a place that shouted magic from every nook and crevice. But before he could think or say anything more, Eriu returned from the fire, bearing her bowl brimming full of rich, thick stew. She set it down in the center of the table, then took a golden spoon and served them both. She filled their trenchers, then put a smaller portion into her own, and finally sat down opposite them.

"Eat," she said. "'Tis your favorite."

Up to that point, Conor's favorite meal had been his mother's venison stew, slowly steamed over a long fire, thickened with gravy and flavorful herbs. But Eriu was right. This was his favorite, though he'd never eaten it before, and had no idea what was in it.

Nevertheless, after the first bite, he reached for the loaf of hot bread resting on the table and tore off chunks, the better to dip and soak the thick broth. He stabbed the point of his knife again and again into the soup and crammed dripping chunks of tender meat into his suddenly ravenous gullet.

Fergus, who had sworn that nothing from this land would pass his lips, ate with even greater frenzy, using his fingers to scoop out particularly succulent pieces. He chewed so quickly, his mouth so full, that crumbs and bits dribbled down his chin and dropped onto the table.

"You must be hungry," Eriu said. "And him too. He eats even better than you."

Fergus's eyes gleamed, and he nodded his head in happy agreement, though he never stopped chewing. But Conor, after his first rush of famished hunger was sated, found himself hungry for something else. And so, though he continued to work his way steadily toward the bottom of his trencher, he found space in his labor to speak a few words.

"I'm sure you have mistaken me for someone else," he said, "so I hope you will forgive me my questions. But can you tell me who you are, and what you do, and where is this place? I've never been anywhere half so wonderful." He paused, then glanced at her, feeling a slow burn rise in his cheeks. "Or seen anyone half so beautiful, either."

"Ah, your tongue is still as golden as your hair, bright warrior," she said softly.

As he cleaned the last scraps out of his trencher, Conor wondered who she thought he was. She seemed so certain that they knew each other . . . and perhaps knew each other more intimately than simple friendship.

Once again, his eyes strayed toward the bed arrayed so invitingly on the other side of the room. But no, he really didn't know her, no matter what she thought, and to take advantage of her mistake would be twice evil—once for the deed, and again for the deception. Nevertheless, his thoughts strayed pleasantly, even as his gaze remained locked on her.

"Fergus," she said. "You eat as you always do, like a starving hog. You will eat it all. Shall I start another kettle for you?"

Her words sounded like an insult, but they didn't feel like one, more like the bantering between old, dear friends. And Fergus seemed to take them that way as well. He looked up at her, gravy dripping from his chin, and grinned. "I could eat your cooking for days, lady, though it would be for the pleasure alone." He leaned back in his seat and patted his rounded belly. "But I am full enough."

She smiled at him. "You needn't leave my table until you are done, but wait, and I will bring you other things."

With that she stood and walked away, then returned after a moment with a great basket filled to bursting with creamy yellow cheeses, with fist-sized lumps of butter, with apples that glowed a perfect, ripe redness, golden pears, peaches all wrapped in velvet down. She took a fresh loaf of nutty bread from the hearth and added it to the bounty. Both men pushed aside their trenchers and dug vigorously into this new repast. Conor felt a curious heat begin to rise in his belly, fill his chest, and paint a fevered glow onto his cheeks and brow. He ate until he thought he might never eat again, and even then found space in which to tuck a final apple.

Across from him, Fergus let out a soft groan as he sprawled backwards, his belly before him like an overfilled wagon. "Lady, I've never eaten like this before, and I doubt I ever will again. I can hardly move!"

"It is written that the way to a warrior's heart lies through his stomach," Eriu said softly, though she stared at Conor, not Fergus, as she spoke. "Doubtless after doing such great deeds at the table, Fergus, you must be exhausted. If you desire rest, there are fragrant hay-mows in the barn, and soft blankets if you wish them."

Her message was plain enough. Fergus was invited to take his leave, but she'd said nothing of Conor himself. She didn't need to. The message in her eyes seemed plain enough to him.

Fergus noticed none of it. All his native caution and wariness had fallen away. His eyelids floated at half-mast, and his broad, satisfied smile betrayed a torpid happiness with everything else.

"Fat old hog," Conor said fondly, but even this jibe brought no response beyond a half nod.

The fire in the great pit snapped and popped comfortingly, sending off a breath of sweet-smelling smoke—so much, in fact, that the air within the cottage began to grow thick and hazy. Conor felt a wonderful lassitude sink into his tired muscles, till it seemed an impossible task even to lift a hand, let alone remove himself to the barn.

"Shall I show you the way, Fergus?" Eriu asked. "Rest will soothe your fears and smooth the weariness from your bones."

Fergus's stupefied expression didn't change, but he began to rise, so slowly it seemed that every movement was a mighty effort. He stood swaying before them. "No, lady, I can find the way."

Conor heard a small sound from high above, and looked up. Again he saw a flicker of movement, but this time he saw the source. The same hoodie crow he'd seen before sat perched at the edge of the smoke-streaked roof-beam, bright black eyes peering down at him. As he watched, the crow slowly opened its horny beak, revealing a bright yellow gullet.

A prick of fear pierced the soft shell that had enfolded him, and once again Conor thought of memory and deception. Eriu was beautiful—even more beautiful than the girl he'd loved and lost so brutally—but whatever plans she had were based on her misunderstanding. And though maybe some men could cheerfully take advantage of her mistake and never think twice about it, Conor couldn't.

The crow closed his beak, though his beady regard never wavered. Conor pushed back his own bench and stood. Eriu stared at him, surprise on her face.

"Where do you go, Golden Hair?"

Conor yawned and stretched widely. "You're right, lady. Fergus and I have a long journey before us, and a good night's sleep will be all to the good. No, you needn't get up. As Fergus says, we can find the way."

"You're leaving me here? Alone?"

Was it his imagination, he wondered, or was there a sudden hint of anger in her tone? Yes, those vertical lines were back above her nose, and her eyebrows now down-slanted. But he shored his resolve.

"I must, lady. Though it would be wonderful to sit and . . . talk . . . for a while, we must be going on soon. So I will thank you once again for your great kindness, and then we will take our leave until the morn."

"There is no morning in this place," she said flatly. "Only the night and the noon. As you well know."

And with that she also stood, brushed her hands against her skirts, and faced him. The smile was gone from her lips, and a darker light uncoiled itself in her eyes. "And once again you leave me, as you have before."

"No, lady, don't task me on it, I beg you. You have been more kind than you needed to be. But I fear we trespass on your courtesy, and I can't do that. We'll just take ourselves off now . . ."

"Yes, go then! Though you may find Eriu's cottage harder to leave behind than you expect. Sleep well!"

With that she turned away and walked to the fireplace and stood silent, her back stiff, her chin high and unmoving.

"Lady . . ."

"Go!"

Conor sighed. As usual, nothing he did, no matter how good the reason for it, seemed to turn out well. "Come, Fergus," he said at last.

But he paused on the door-stoop and said, "I thank you again, lady."

She didn't turn, but she did answer: "We will see."

The last thing he heard as he left her cottage was a sudden rush of wings, and again a single harsh caw.

The hoodie crow.

—3—

Two broad wooden doors stood wide, offering a welcoming entrance to the barn at the back of the cottage. The dun cow had come back to the fence, and watched them calmly as they moved past. Everything seemed very slow: the cow's switching tail, the cool breath of breeze from the distant mountains, their own halting footsteps. Even the mingled light from the sun and the stars—a clear, limpid wash touched with gold—was thick and soft and dreamlike.

From the barn issued the scent of freshly mown hay. They went inside, and found stacks of soft blankets piled there, and pillows fluffed with feathers. It was dimmer here, full of shadows that soothed and quieted. Conor suddenly realized that the buzzing in his head had vanished.

"Well, old bear, so much for your vows," he said, as he spread out blankets on a soft mound of straw.

"Eh, what?"

"You swore to eat nothing on this island, not

fruit nor animal, nor drink of water. But the only thing you didn't devour at the table was the table itself."

Fergus blinked, then slowly shook his head. "So tired, Conor. I need to sleep now. I do."

Fergus lay down on his own bed, put his hands behind his head, and stared up at the ceiling. The head of the dun cow appeared in a window that gave off onto the kraal. She stared at them with vague attentiveness, as if interested in their doings, but only mildly so.

Conor arranged his blankets into a luxuriant, fragrant mound, and lay down himself. The hay enfolded him. It was, he imagined, like settling into a bed made of clouds.

"Fergus, I don't want to sound disloyal, but I think she's even more beautiful than Claire . . . and I never thought any woman of flesh and blood would seem so to me."

The cow moved her head as if agreeing, then turned away and vanished from the window.

"Fergus?"

The only reply he got was a sudden fusillade of Fergus's snores—and that was the last thing he heard before he drifted off, the beauty of Eriu floating in his mind like an impossible vision.

—— 4 ——

He didn't know what woke him. Something had changed. Maybe there was a sound, or a shift in the air.

Everything was very still. He sat up on his bed and looked over at his companion. Fergus's eyes were closed, though his mustache quivered with the force of his snoring. Yet no sounds issued from the old warrior's open mouth.

For some reason, nothing about that seemed strange. The light in the barn was clear and gray, and full of silver shadows. Conor stood up. He felt a pull deep in his bones, a hidden summons. He began to drift slowly toward the door, and then through them, out into the courtyard. As he passed the kraal he noticed it was empty. He looked up, and saw that the sky was now equally divided between light and night. The line of demarcation between the two was as sharp as a knife cut. And when he looked down, he saw that half the stedd was in day, the other half in darkness. This curious arrangement neatly bisected Eriu's cottage, dividing her front door in twain.

But he felt no alarm. It was as if this was how things were, how they should be, how they had been for a time longer than time itself.

He stepped onto the paving stones and came up to the door. But as he raised his hand to the bell, the door opened silently. He entered the cottage, and found himself in the same room as before. But the light that flowed out to greet him was thick and golden as fresh honey. A thousand candles winked and flickered and glowed, and filled the welcoming gloom with a net of shadows.

He stepped across the threshold. As he did so, he heard a long sighing, as if something hidden had drawn secret breath. He turned and saw her on the bed. Her hair lay in a great black fan all around her, like a shining blanket spread out to display her own perfect beauty.

Her lake-haunted eyes gleamed in that gloaming, cups spilling over with emerald fire.

"Lady . . ." he whispered.

She spread her arms, and the milky sweetness of her form lay open before him, pliant and inviting.

"I've been waiting. Wondering if you would come. Wondering if you had truly forgotten me."

"No, I have not, lady. I will never forget you."

"Come to me, then . . ."

It seemed as if a slow, warm wind now plucked at him, urging him onward even as it lifted his clothes away, and caressed his naked skin with a thousand invisible fingers. As in a dream he went to her.

She smelled of musk and a dewy sweat, and her lips tasted of apples. Conor groaned.

"Ah, lady . . ."

"Oh, golden-haired boy, I knew you could not forget Eriu. I knew it."

The world swirled away.

—5—

How long they sought each other in that bed Conor never knew, for time itself seemed banished from him.

Like the coals of some fire undimmed, their light rose and fell, rose and fell. At once she smelled of honey and ginger, then of forgotten snowy winters, then of deep wells never before drunk, then earthy and green, like fresh-cut grass.

He sank into her gaze as into still waters, and though he didn't breathe, his lungs were full of her, his chest strained with the silent beat of his own heart.

It was a great silence, yet he heard many times the rush of wings, or the cry of distant, lonely wind. White seabirds whirled and cried above secret oceans, filling him with a sadness so sweet it was indistinguishable from joy.

He walked through a mighty sunrise, and then sat on stone beneath a sky of stars so clear he knew their lamps had been lit only moments before. The world was new, untouched, and their footprints in the grass beneath a moonless, sunless sky, were as new as the world, and as old as the First Spirits.

She took him along the hidden paths that only the Sidhe knew, and in his ears wailed a thin siren-cry, so that his heart was taken in many snares, and he neither knew nor cared whether he would ever be free again.

"Ah! Ah! Golden Hair!" she shouted again and again, until her voice was a single long peal of thunder, and he was drowning in it.

"If this be a dream," he whispered, "then let me sleep forever."

—6—

*"Conor!"*

He thought that shout was loud, but it was far away, and easy to ignore. All around him swirled silver clouds, and flickering between them fires that both heated and soothed him, and he had no wish to leave them.

*"Conor, damn you, wake up!"*

Slowly the clouds shifted, battered by that distant cry. The sound of it seemed to come from a particular direction . . . there. And now the fires were dying, the red glow dimming away, growing cold.

"No . . ." he muttered. "No . . . I can't."

*"Conor!"*

Then his world shook. Great cracks of lightning split the silver clouds, and blasted the fires into nothingness. He stretched out his hands, trying to re-gather what was now vanishing, and—

"Conor, open your eyes! Are your senses gone, lad? Wake up!"

"Whu . . . ? What?"

Something clubbed him across the jaw, knocking his eyelids up.

"What? Fergus? Stop *hitting* me!"

Fergus's craggy features hung before him, so close he could smell the old warrior's breath.

"Are you back, lad? Is it you? Do you know me?"

Weakly Conor tried to push him away. "Of course I know you."

He raised himself up on his elbows and looked blearily around. He was lying spraddled on a rumpled bed, his nakedness half-covered with a soft blanket. Across the room a fire leaped and danced beneath a great black kettle.

"What? Fergus, how did I get here? I went to sleep in the barn. You were there . . ."

Slowly the look of deep concern began to fade from Fergus's face. He stepped back from the bed. "Yes, lad, I remember it." Then he grinned wickedly. "But from the evidence before my own eyes, and yours too, you didn't stay in the hay-mow long."

Conor glanced down. "Oh."

"Yes, indeed, oh, laddie."

A sudden wave of embarrassment sent his cheeks flushing as he scrabbled to pull the blanket up to his neck. Fergus chuckled and lifted something soft, shapeless, but familiar.

"You left your shirt and breeks strewn all around," he said. "Maybe you'd like them now?" With a laugh he tossed them at Conor's head.

"Turn around. Don't look."

"Huh. As if I hadn't seen it all before."

As Conor struggled into his clothes, a sharp sound from above drew his eyes. The hoodie crow was there, its shiny black gaze fixed on him.

"Hawrk!" the crow said.

"Oh, shut up," Conor muttered. He pulled up his britches and hitched his belt tight, then swung his legs to the floor and stood.

"Conor?" Fergus said softly.

Conor swung around.

The hag stood silently in the doorway, watching them.

# EIGHT

## THE SADNESS OF SWEET PARTINGS

—1—

Conor recoiled from the hideous figure that stood like a dark stone in the doorway, fear choking his heart at the sight of her. A bent and crooked crone, her skin like seamed granite, lips of cracked leather pulled back and snarling to reveal teeth stained with ancient blood. Her black eyes bulged beneath a tangled nest of hair the color of a sick man's piss. She leaned on a twisted stave, which she grasped with fingers like claws. Atop the staff perched a crow, at first seeming but a carving of the wood, until Conor saw its red eyes blink.

His breath stopped cold in his throat. He tried to scream, but his chest was full of ice. "Ah . . ." he groaned. "Ah . . ."

Fergus too seemed stricken with a terrible fear, and stood unmoving, his eyes starting from his skull. The hag eyed them, then whispered in a voice soft with liquid foulness, "What's the matter, Golden Hair? Do you not know me?"

The sound of her words was like a long scrape of doom across Conor's spine. Once again he tried to speak, but the terror that wafted off the hag in dark breaths unstrung his muscles and turned his bones to jelly, and he could only stand and listen to the inward shriek of his own horror.

Slowly she raised her staff, and in a single motion deliberate as the chop of a headsman's axe, slammed its iron-shod butt onto the wooden floor.

And she was gone. High overhead, lost and distant in the rafters, came the mocking scream of a hoodie crow. With that horrid cry, though it froze the heart, somehow the spell was broken, and they were released from their terror.

"Did . . . did you see that?" Conor whispered.

Fergus was slowly straightening, running his hands across his chest as if feeling for wounds. "Yes, lad, I saw it."

They stared at each other.

"What . . . ?" Conor breathed.

Fergus shook his head. "I don't know. How could I know? This is a magic island. A place not meant for the likes of us. You found yourself a pretty girl. But pretty girls don't bar monsters." His brows lowered. "I fear that sometimes they even may be the same."

"What? That horror wasn't Eriu! Have your eyes become clouded in your old age?"

Fergus gave off feeling himself for injury—though from the expression on his face, his injuries, if any, might have been deeper than the flesh—and shook his head. "My vision may grow weaker with time, but my heart doesn't. That was a monster, Conor. Old lady death. And she was here, as if she knew this place well. What do you say?"

Conor shook his head stubbornly. "Not Eriu. She is sweet, and loving, and . . ."

"Why, thank you, Golden Hair," Eriu said, stepping across the threshold, a basket laden with fruit in her hands, her cheeks pinkly dappled, her eyes green with laughter.

Fergus started back, his hands groping reflexively for the sword across his back, but she ignored him. She walked toward the fire, the hem of her skirts whispering across the planked floorboards, regal as any queen.

She laughed at Fergus as she passed him by. "Would you take sword to me, mighty warrior?"

Fergus let his hands fall and, cheeks flaming, mumbled something and turned away. But it was clear the witchment that had held him at table the night before was gone, and he was back to his old suspicious wariness.

He glanced at Conor. "Time we were going, lad. I'll get our gear ready and wait outside for you."

Eriu set down her load on the broad hearth, then straightened her skirts as she stood. She patted her black hair back from her white forehead and said, "What's wrong with you, Conor? You look pale as a winter moon."

"I . . . uh . . . there was a woman. An old woman . . . she came to the door. But she's gone now."

"An old woman? It must have been my sister.

She visits me here on occasion." Eriu's lips curled in a soft smile. "Why? Did she frighten you?"

Conor took a breath. "She was horrible, Eriu. She made me think of death, and all things rotten and decayed."

Eriu held her hands out to the flames dancing on the hearth. The light of the fire cast a ruddy glow across her cheeks. "She doesn't show herself often, you know. And only in certain circumstances."

Conor moved toward her. "Certain circumstances?"

"Yes, oftentimes warriors see her on the battlefield. She is an omen."

"An omen of what?"

Eriu turned to face him. "Why, of death, of course. If you have truly met her, how else could you think?"

Conor closed his eyes. Once again he felt the chill, ghastly breath of that apparition wafting over him. He reached out and took Eriu's hands.

"Lady, I don't know who you are. But I think you must not be exactly what you seem. Yet you look to me as a maid, young and more beautiful than any other woman."

She placed one fingertip across his lips, silencing him. Her eyes gleamed up at him.

"Any other woman, Golden Hair? Even your Claire?"

Conor gave a start. "Claire? How do you know about Claire?"

Eriu smiled her enigmatic smile. "It is mine to know much, and see things far away both in time and in the world of men. I know of Claire, Conor. How not?"

"Then I fear I've betrayed myself—and her too."

"No, there is no treachery in you. Claire is a mortal woman, and you have remained faithful to her. For my caresses soil not mortal flesh in any way, and my hands are clean, and my kisses sweet."

As he stared into her eyes, Conor knew this was true, and a great grief lifted away from him. For he understood the secret knowledge of his own heart, that whatever had befallen in the night before, he had not bedded a mortal woman.

"Who are you?" he asked her at last.

"Do you not know me, Golden Hair?"

Slowly he nodded his head up and down, for in that moment it seemed he did know her, or remember her, from some past time. But he didn't know how or when.

Yet his reply seemed to both soothe and please her, for she suddenly smiled, and the brightness of that lifted up his heart, and all his fears were swept away.

He bowed to her, and kissed the tips of her fingers. "Lady," he whispered. "You are too high and grand for me, and though I desired to stay with you forever, I cannot. For I would burn in your fires, and be lost. And I have a quest I cannot leave off, not even for the joy that waits in your embrace. I hope you can forgive me, just as I hope I can forgive myself."

She stepped away from him. "You are a proud man, Conor." Her gaze sharpened on him, full of speculation. "And I know you now, better than I thought. In you lies the holy power of *avatar,* he-who-is-shaped-in-the-form-of-another. But you are not the other, though I thought so at first. Yet as to that other you are a reflection, like a bright mirror, and your light will return again and again in the worlds of men. That is your long doom, though you know it not yet."

Then she came to him, and kissed him on the lips, and he remembered the heat of her for the rest of his days, for he was marked by her, and would never forget the taste of her sweetness.

After a time she released him, and stepped back and said, "Tell me of your quest, Conor. It may be that I can be of some service to it. And for you I would do that, in token of the thing we have shared together."

Then for an instant she revealed herself to him, and he saw her as she truly was: tall and fair, with a silver crown in her hair. And she strode across the night, scattering the stars from her hand, and in her van the sun, and at her back the moon.

But only for an instant, as the true sight of her was beyond the hope of mortal flesh, except for the smallest of glimpses. Conor staggered back, and she caught him, and held him up.

"Do not fear me, Conor," she said. "Your end lies not at my hand, but at another's. And your time will not end in simple fate, nor even in long doom, though the last of your tale is hidden even from me. Yet I will help you in all that you do, both now and in the countless tomorrows of your days.

Now sit, and refresh yourself before you go, and tell me of the quest that has been laid upon you."

She lifted her basket again, and he saw that it was overflowing with many fruits and rich, golden cheeses. She led him back to the table and sat down with him, and they ate together and talked for a long time.

He told her all that had happened, of the Land and the curse on it, and of the Spear, and the great wizards, Galen, Longinus, the child Blas, and Myrddin. When he spoke this last name, her eyebrows went up and she raised one hand.

"Hold! Tell me more of this one, this magician who calls himself Myrddin, who dwells at the far edge of the Sundering Water."

Conor told her everything he could remember, about both Myrddin the Mage and the Castle of Glass that was his home. Eriu sat silent, listening, her chin resting on her hand, her eyes closed. When he had finished, she opened her eyes, and once again he saw the dangerous flash hidden deep within them, unless she should choose to reveal it.

Though she watched him, at first she said nothing, until he asked her, "Lady, is something wrong? I have not lied, but told you everything that I know. Will you tell me what are your thoughts? For it seems to me you do have thoughts on the matter."

"The matter of Myrddin the great wizard? Yes, I do. Although it is not entirely clear, I believe I do know him. If he is the one I think he is, then your peril is both high and deep. For as you are a mirror of another, so is he bonded and bound beyond his own mortal flesh, which he wears like a cloak to conceal the truth beneath. Beware of him, Conor! He is not what he seems, nor what you think."

At this warning Conor felt a knife of fear pierce his heart, for he was afraid that his quest was for naught, and that Myrddin had lied to him, seeking to use him for purposes he could not see. But when he said this, Eriu shook her head.

"No, he has told you the truth, or at least a part of it," she said. "But you are right. He does have purposes of his own that are beyond the quest he has set for you."

"Can you tell me what they are, lady?"

She seemed about to speak, but she paused for a long time, and finally said, "I cannot. Or, rather, I will not, for the one who calls himself Myrddin plays at a role far beyond your ken. Indeed, it concerns the long weavings of the Sidhe themselves, and though I could gainsay it, I will not."

"But am I bidden to fail, then? Is my quest for nothing, and the curse will not be lifted from the Land?"

She took his hands in hers. "As to your failure, that is up to you. Your strength and your heart will determine whether you succeed, and indeed you may fail. But if you return to Myrddin with what he seeks of you, then he will lift the curse from your Land, and all will be well there, at least for a time."

At these words, Conor once again felt a rush of joy, for there was at least a chance that he might succeed in his quest. As for the rest, he understood little, except that he was somehow involved with doings beyond his comprehension. But he was young, and strong, and trusted in himself, and so was less dismayed than he might have been.

"What of my friends, Tully and Catlin? They lie in enchanted sleep, hard as stones, on this side of the river."

"Yes," she said, "that is the sleep of the Sidhe, and it will not harm nor change them as long as they are caught within it."

"But how can I release them?"

She regarded him sadly. "Ah, Conor, you do not know. They may not thank you for being awakened. For though their flesh lies frozen and cold, their spirits wander free in the Golden Isle, and they are with the Deathless, blessed beyond mortal hope. Many might wish that such a fate would never end."

"But I must try," he told her.

"Yes, I suppose you must." She sat back from him, and sighed heavily. "I see many threads leaping here, from warp to woof, and though the hands of the weavers are plain to me, I would not disturb the shape of the pattern they make. Much lies on you, Conor, on your courage, and strength, and on the choices you will make. This is my prophecy, and my help. You must mount three tests, and surmount them. You will face the Questing Beast, the Hall of the Four Watchers, and the Guarded Lord Asleep. It is the head of him who sleeps I must have to help you. Bring it to me, and I will show you the Cauldron, which you may take to Myrddin and so fulfill your quest. But these are no small tasks, and I would help you as I can, for the sake of the night we have shared."

Then she reached into the front of her dress and withdrew a shining gem, which hung from her neck on a silver chain. She handed the jewel to him. "This is Ang-lorion, a fairy-stone, made long ago in the smelter of Dagdha, who is named Eochaid Ollathair, the Father of All, and I have hallowed it. Take it and wear it, and know that my thoughts go with you. In times of need, you may find use for it, for it is my lamp, and in times of darkness it will light your way."

Conor stared in wonder at the gift she had given him. The stone called Ang-lorion rested on his palm in a shimmering puddle of light, gleaming with a white fire, though he could see that deep within its heart was also green, which was the color of her eyes.

Carefully he slipped the chain over his head, so that the stone itself rested on his breastbone, nearest to his heart. He could feel it there, seeming to throb in harmony with his heartbeat.

"This is a mighty gift, Eriu," he said. "I will wear it and think of you always."

She smiled then, and said, "Always is a very long time, Conor, though for your part, you may speak the truth unknowing. But I will say that as long as you do wear my stone, I will be with you, and you will ever be in my thoughts."

"Who are you, lady?"

But she only laughed, and stood up, and said, "No more questions, Conor. I have told you what I can, and what I must. Someday hence you will remember what you already know, but I don't hold that forgetting against you. Now it is time for you to go. Your gruff liege-man waits outside, growing gruffer, I suspect, with each passing moment."

Conor smiled. "Yes, I suppose he is. But he is brave, and trusty, and true, and I forgive him his gruffness. He is dear to me."

They came to the door and faced each other for the last time. She raised her face to him, and he kissed her, and they stepped apart.

Just as he passed beyond her threshold, he heard her speak, though she murmured and did not look at him.

"Even the gods," she whispered, "may know the sadness of loss."

At her back, hidden in the gloom-cloaked rafters, came the cry of a hoodie crow: Cawrk!

She closed the door.

"Finally!" Fergus said, coming up. "What were you talking about so long?"

Conor turned and faced him, a dreamy smile on his face. "She said you were a grump."

Fergus snorted at that. "Then she was at least right about one thing. Are you ready?"

"I am."

"Then let's go."

And so they turned their faces toward the Mountains of Guard, which crowded at the feet of Ilmarin the Mighty, and left behind the sweet-running spring and the homely cottage of the lady Eriu, and all that had happened there.

Only the dun cow watched them go.

—2—

The path wound toward the mountains, growing fainter as it rose, and finally dying entirely as they entered a land of jagged boulders, dark-skinned stones whose edges and corners cut like knives.

The deeper they marched into these swelling scarps, the darker the sky grew overhead, until the blue dome of daylight was only a bare gentle haze above the horizon at their back. It also grew steadily more cold, the wind as sharp and hard as the stones over which they climbed. Conor was glad of his cloak, and drew it tighter around his neck.

"Three tasks, eh?" Fergus said. He was sweating as he clambered up and down, and there were deep scores on his palms, some crusted and scabbed over, some fresh and lined with blood. Nevertheless, he continued, breaking trail for Conor, who came after him.

"She named three, yes."

"The Questing Beast doesn't sound very promising," Fergus grunted. "Watch your step, lad!"

Conor's right foot came down on a flat plate of dark shale that gave way as soon as he put his weight on it. His hands flew up as his feet slipped out from beneath him. The Gae Bolga went whipping from his grasp to land with a great clang below, and he followed, tumbling and bouncing, with Fergus scrambling after him.

"Whoa, are you all right?" Fergus heaved him up and brushed him off, while Conor stood shaking his head, listening to the sound of bells in his ears, and marveling at how the world was spinning.

"Uh . . ."

"Nasty little gash there," Fergus said, licking the pad of one broad thumb and running it alongside the edge of Conor's left eye. "Hold still!"

Conor winced as Fergus brought his thumb away. Though the light of noon was far behind them now, the blaze of the stars was also very bright, though in their light fresh blood gleamed black as oil.

"I'm bleeding," Conor said, wondering when his head would stop whirling.

Fergus cleaned away the blood with the hem of his cloak, and after a moment's work said, "It's slowing now. I think it will be well. It doesn't looked deep, and after all, it's only a head wound. In your case, that means no danger at all. Might as well take a whack at a brick."

Conor was still dizzy, but he laughed at that, remembering Myrddin making the same joke about Fergus. As he thought of the magician, a curious lassitude, of which he had not even been aware, was lifted from him. And as that curtain lifted, so did the enchantments that Eriu herself had laid upon him, and he saw all that had happened to him in her place suddenly plain.

"Lad, what's the matter? You're trembling, though it's only a scratch. Here, sit down before you fall down."

Conor went to his knees, and Fergus helped him to sit with his back against a low boulder.

"You've gone pale as a fish belly! Are you wounded elsewhere? Do you feel pain, a broken bone perhaps?"

But Conor only shook his head, as if both frightened and weighed down with a great weariness. "I feel pain, my friend, but no bones are broken. Only my heart, maybe."

Fergus grunted, and sat down beside him. They stayed so for a long time, neither man speaking, while their breath rose in chill clouds around them, for it was growing much colder.

Finally Fergus shifted and spoke. "What happened, lad? You were all right, but now you look as you did that morning when you walked through the ashes of our vanished home, among the hewed corpses of your family."

"I have lost something great, Fergus," Conor said slowly, "though I did not know at the time what it was. But it is gone now, and I have nothing left of it but this."

He reached beneath his shirt and took out the stone named Ang-lorion. Fergus saw it and drew his breath sharply, for under starlight the fairy-stone blazed with the light of many stars, and cast their shadows all about against the folded rocks.

"She gave that to you?"

"Yes."

"Put it away, Conor, for its light burns my eyes."

Conor nodded, and shielded it again beneath his clothes. But his eyes gleamed with sadness even in the renewed dark, and his expression remained downfallen.

"That is a mighty gift, Conor."

"Yes, but a token only, of the greater gift I have lost. Oh, Fergus! I have paid more than I guessed, and my purse is empty now."

But Fergus only shook his head, and said, "That is the way of quests, lad. But come, are you feeling better now?" He put one hand on Conor's shoulder as he turned and stared up the forbidding walls still before them. "This is a bitter place, barren and cold, and I would find a better one in which to take some rest."

"Take my hand, then, and help me up. I am weak, and I don't know if I will ever find my strength again."

So Fergus raised him, for he was always the strong right arm of the line from whence Conor, son of Derek, had sprung. And in the light of the ancient stars, which were the first lights to break darkness before the coming of dawn in the morning of the world, many things were revealed to him, and he saw his own long doom. But he feared it not, and felt a great joy instead, and he laughed as he lifted Conor up. For he knew then that not all fates were withered before promise, not the least his own.

They went on.

—3—

They climbed onward for a long time, though without the sun or the moon to serve as marks, they had no way of numbering the hours beneath the stars. Finally even Fergus's great strength began to wane, while Conor's own vitality had not fully returned to him.

"We must stop awhile. I can't go on much longer," Fergus said. He paused, and wiped a sheen of sweat from his gleaming skull, and shook his head as he stared upward along their way, hidden though it was. "It looks as if it goes on forever, Conor. From far off, these mountains seemed only mountains, though high and sharp. But as we go on, the stones themselves seem to stretch beneath our feet, and with each step the way grows longer. I fear that we could spend the sum of our lives climbing here, and find ourselves no closer to the top of these bitter hills, for we are caught again in some evil enchantment."

Conor turned and looked back down the line of the journey they had already made, and saw that they were indeed very high above the darkling plain below. They had come far, and now stood in the middle air above a vast darkness, which spread to the lowermost hem of the stars that made a curtain above the distant horizon. The light of the noonday was also gone now, and only the dark remained. When he turned back to seek the tops of the Mountains of Guard, they loomed before him still, high and distant, though shrouded behind shadows, and they were no closer than they had been before. Or so it seemed.

"Then we will stop for a while and eat, and sleep, and take counsel after we have rested. We're both tired, and maybe our minds are clouded, and hope hidden from us. Perhaps we will see clearer-eyed later."

They found a tiny plateau, no wider than a few men might stand on, but broad enough for them to lie at length. From the stones grew small, gnarled bushes, with thick leaves and tiny berries that gleamed black under the sun. Some of these had died, and the berries shriveled. Fergus hacked at them with his sword and cut them loose.

This wood burned with an aromatic smoke that filled their small grot with the scent of dewberries and sandalwood, so they had a bit of warmth and flickering light in the midst of all the gloom.

And though they knew it not, Eriu came to the door of her cottage far away, and with her longsight she descried their light as a faint golden gleam against the hem of Ilmarin, and she smiled to herself.

As before, the contents of their packs had renewed themselves. Fergus took out cheese and bread and fruit, and a flagon of beer miraculously cold, and they laid out a repast before their fire, and banished, for a moment at least, the drear sameness of their trek.

But as they ate, Conor thought of the source of their bounty, the magician Myrddin, and what Eriu had spoken regarding that wizard.

"Eriu said that I must beware of Myrddin," he remarked.

Fergus, his mouth full, grunted. He swallowed and said, "Then I think better of the lass, for she says nothing more than I have said already."

"So you say 'I told you so,' is that it?" Conor replied, grinning.

For once, Fergus didn't see any humor. He nodded. "That one is dangerous, Conor, and though I don't know how much truth is in him, or not, he works his own purposes. And I don't think he's truly of mortal flesh, nor does he care overmuch what happens to the mortals he does use in the consummation of his wiles. We are his tools, Conor, or so he thinks."

Conor began to feel drowsy, with the comforting crackle of the fire in his ears, and his belly full, and sweet smells filling his nose. But as he drifted off, he remembered the things Eriu had told him, and he said, "Yes, he does seek to use us. But I believe we both have our own dooms, separate from all that he does, or hopes for. And though our goals may lie together for a while, in the end we will go on different ways, and his magics will fail against us. Yet in the meantime we do remain together, and will serve each other, whether trusty or not."

"Let us hope so, then," Fergus replied. "Though hope seems a strange and distant thing, here among the stones."

Conor lay back, his head pillowed on his pack, and stared up at the stars above, and felt the silent throb of a different star upon his breast.

"There is always hope, Fergus," he said at last, just before he fell into a dreamless sleep. "Hope is the doom of mortal men, our gift, and guard, and goad, for it was given to us at the Beginning, before even these stars above us were first lit against the dark."

"But hope may fail," Fergus said.

"Not always," Conor replied.

# NINE

## ON ILMARIN'S KNEE

### —1—

Conor and Fergus woke to night, as it had been before they slept, for the stars did not change nor darkness lessen in the place where they were.

Conor sat up and stretched, trying to work the chill and stiffness from his muscles. Though his body was slow, he found his mind clear, and renewed of purpose, and his weariness gone. The fire at his feet had burned down to cold ash. He took his sword and cut at the few remaining dry stalks that grew in the cracks about them, and piled this kindling together for a new blaze. But he had no flint stones. He went to Fergus and shook his shoulder.

"Wake up, Fergus, and help me light our fire. A bit of warmth and a bite of food would go well before we start off again."

Fergus groaned, coming awake beneath the stars, but after some spluttering and eye rubbing and a wide yawn or two, he set to work, chipping sparks onto the wood that was prepared. They ate quickly, without much talk, and when they were done, they packed as before, though their kits had not grown smaller.

"At least we keep on eating, eh," Fergus said as he hoisted his sack to his shoulders.

Conor, doing likewise, nodded. "Our rations may be magical, but they fill our bellies. Not everything given to us by Myrddin has been chancy, or full of tricks."

"But enough has," Fergus replied, turning to stare at the bleakness rising ahead. A wind was blowing again from that direction, strong and steady, and it nipped through even their warm cloaks. Fergus scuffed out their small cook-fire and piled stones on the ashes. "I'll miss the warmth," he said sadly. "And the light. For where we go now, I fear the darkness only grows deeper, and without a path we will lose our direction entirely."

Conor finished cinching tight his load and adjusting his sword scabbard across his back. He took up the Gae Bolga, meaning to use it again as a staff, but when he raised it up, he felt the scrape of stone against his breast, and remembered what he wore there.

"In times of darkness it will light your way," Eriu had told him. This was surely a time of darkness, and their way was hidden.

Conor parted his cloak, and reached beneath his shirt to feel the hard shape of the stone.

"Fergus, you have broken the path for me, and now I must do the same for you. Here, take the Gae Bolga."

Fergus did so, and said, "What are you thinking, Conor?"

"You must take my hand, and walk behind me. You said the light of Ang-lorion burned your eyes, so you will keep them shut tight, and I will lead you while the stone lights our way."

Fergus was troubled, fearing the power of the stone, but he could think of nothing else to do. "Maybe there is good luck in that light, Conor, but it is too harsh and bright for me, and how much good is in a blaze that blinds and burns?"

"Maybe enough," Conor said. "It doesn't harm me, and I see clearly in its gleam."

"Go ahead, then. I will hold your hand and follow."

So that is what they did. Fergus took the Gae Bolga in his right hand, put his left into Conor's right, and closed his eyes tight against the fire he feared. Conor lifted the chain from his neck and revealed Ang-lorion's light once again, as he had before, holding the stone before him like a lantern.

And as before, Ang-lorion kindled a great light beneath the stars, for captured within it was the light of the first stars, and it cried upward to its brothers. From it sprang a wide beam, hard and pure, that picked out every nook and crevice in the stone, and revealed all that was there.

By that light Conor saw a path he had not seen before. Thin and shrinking, but now plainly visible, it led upward, meandering a bit but always turning back toward their distant goal, night-crowned Ilmarin, King of Mountains.

So they set off, one leading the other, and both led by the Lamp of Eriu, whose light would never fail unless the world and the stars beyond should also fail. And it was bearing this great fire, which was a beacon and a warning before them, that they finally surmounted the stony lands, and came up at last onto the broad flat plains of Adamantillon, of which the forgotten songs sang.

This was in itself a mighty deed, for on that wide shelf no foot of living man had ever trod, until, lit by the chained light of stars, Conor and Fergus came there.

Beyond reared Ilmarin's peak, tallest of mountains that the Powers had raised in the beginning of time; and also, caught in his tangled roots, a fiery glimmer that was the Four-Cornered Castle, the Horned Keep that was their goal.

As Conor hooded his fairy-light, Fergus opened his eyes.

"'Tis very far away, lad," he said.

"But closer than it was," Conor replied. "And our path is now clear toward it."

"So it is," Fergus agreed, and they set off again.

—2—

Where their trail before had been rough and broken, and choked with great stones, Fergus and Conor now found their way across the wide ledge of Adamantillon much easier, for the land was level here, like a vast table covered thickly with tiny stones. As they walked, their boots raised small grinding sounds, and after a time Conor halted, and stooped down.

"What is this, Fergus?" he said. He scooped up a full palm of the gritty stuff, and let it trail out in a glittering stream. Hard and bright those kernels were, and full of sharp edges and points.

"Like cinders," Fergus said, also stooping. "In the Land there are black stones that burn, which are found near places where oil leaks thickly from the earth. When those stones are consumed, they leave behind a hard ash, like this stuff."

Conor raised another handful and brought it to his nose. "Yes, I can smell the memory of ancient fires in it, now cold and dead." He let it fall, and stood again, but his expression was creased with worry. "A great burning . . ." he said doubtfully, trying to comprehend what sort of conflagration could level so great a space.

Adamantillon indeed was a wasteland, blasted and burned so that nothing stood above, not tree or stone or any other thing.

"I have heard of mountains that split open, and pour flames like thick honey out of their broken sides," Fergus said.

"Yes, Galen spoke of such," Conor replied. "But he said those peaks gave off great smokes and fumes, and a stench like eggs left out to rot in the sun, and the earth about them trembled constantly. Yet here is the silence of dark graves, and the air is clear as still water."

They gave the question a good bit of thought, but weren't able to discover any explanation for these things, except that in a place of magic they might find much that was new and strange to them, as they already had.

But Fergus, already wary, was even more on guard. "I will walk in front," he said, "and you guard my back, as we did before."

Conor went to the rear and watched in every direction, holding the Gae Bolga in both hands. But all was silent and empty, and the stars gleamed down on them with a harsh light, and they saw nothing.

When they finally stopped to rest and refresh themselves, they sat where they halted, and ate from their packs, and drank beer out of the magical jugs Myrddin had given them. There were no springs here, or wood for burning, or evidence that anything had ever lived or grown in the place. And though they had walked far, the Horned Castle seemed no nearer.

"Maybe I should try the fairy-lamp again," Conor said. "It seemed to shorten the paths that it found, so that we came to an end."

Fergus shook his head. "I feared that light before, Conor, and now I fear it even more, for it would be like a shining beacon, and visible to the furthest edges of this plain. You come to plunder a mighty hoard, and I cannot think it wise to herald the coming of a pair of mortal thieves. Especially when those who watch most likely do so with eyes that are farseeing and without squint or stain."

He paused a moment, thinking further. "Did

your lady say anything of this place, or tell you what you might find?"

"No, she only named my trials, and said I must bring her the head of the Sleeping King from his place within the Four-Cornered Keep."

"His head? You said nothing of that before!"

Conor sighed. "Nor did Myrddin. Myrddin said the Cauldron itself was in the castle, and we should find it there, and bring it to him. But Eriu says instead to bring her the head, and she will show us the Cauldron."

"Riddles! And the two riddlers don't even agree. One says this, and the other says different. How do you propose to reconcile them?"

"I don't know, Fergus. Eriu told me to beware of Myrddin, as I've said. And so have you told me, though I don't know what I'm supposed to do. All warn of others, and how do I know who to trust?"

"I say trust no one, then!"

"Yes, Fergus, but then where are we? If I treat all as liars, then we are doomed, and have nothing to do. But if I do nothing, then Tully and Catlin remain as they are, and the curse also stays upon the Land, and all our hopes are gone."

Fergus could not argue against this, though his mood grew even grimmer. "Trust not in magic, for it is faithless," he muttered.

But Conor, who had until this time said little against Fergus's grumblings, grew angry, for he was weary and his heart ached with the loss he had suffered. "Then what, old man, would you have me do? Return down our path, and go back across the river, and give up everything? I have chosen otherwise, to see this to the end, though I cannot tell what that will be. But my choice need not be yours. If you wish, take half of what we have, and go. I will continue on alone, because my doom is ahead, not behind me."

Fergus was abashed, and bowed his head. "I will follow you, Conor, as I have sworn."

"If you will follow me, then gripe me no more gripes, nor gainsay what I do, but help me." Then his voice softened, and he touched Fergus on one knee. "I know it's hard, old bear, and you are fearful, not just for yourself, but for me and the others. And so am I afraid, caught between a magician and a woman whom I doubt is mortal. But they do agree on one thing: The key to our trial is in that castle before us. So I say we go and get it, and worry about dividing the spoils we find only after we have found them. What do you say? Will you go on with me with a whole heart—and a silent tongue?"

"A silent tongue?" Suddenly Fergus laughed, a great roar that shook the silence that shrouded them, a human sound that seemed out of place, yet greatly welcome. "My tongue will be as silent as your skull is thick. But I will not harp at you any longer, because the time of choice is past, and I have made mine. Maybe I do grumble out of worry, or, as you say, fear. But it does no good, except perhaps to make me feel better."

"Ah, Fergus. You are like a mother to me, then." Conor's grin was white in his face, and his eyes sparkled in the starlight.

Fergus stood up. "Nay, lad, were that so I'd be

kicking your butt from here to the cliffs that guard our distant Land, for getting me into this."

"But you won't." Conor also stood, and busied himself with his pack. "You know, old bear, I love you."

Then Fergus grinned, and answered him, "I love you too, Conor." He paused, his grin growing wider. "Shall we kiss now, as the maidens do?"

They set off, whooping with laughter, and for a time the burdens they carried were the lighter for it. But the sound of their happy cries, so alien to the dark reaches of Adamantillon, went out ahead of them, and betrayed their coming as surely as the light of the Lamp of Eriu would have done.

For the eyes and ears that guarded the Hidden Plain were sharp as knives, and now something ancient and terrible stirred, and woke within its secret lair. And after a time it crawled out into the starlight to discover what had disturbed its long sleep.

—3—

It is told that in the time of the First Dominion, when the Powers who named themselves the Uru-Sidhe, or the Great Flames, walked the earth unclothed, and their light and the light of the stars filled up Avallon Longhome from its deepest wells to its highest peaks, there came at last a time of strife among the Deathless. For on the one hand was Dagdha, the Father of All, and those he counted as minions and vassals, whom he had created in the depths of darkness before the beginning of time. But of his children was also Balor, who was great in power, and eager for more. Of all the children of Dagdha, he was the fairest, and Dagdha loved him the most, though he was a sore trial to him.

Now it came, as the First Dominion of the Powers grew toward its noon, that Dagdha commanded his queen, Morrighan the Bright and Terrible, to bring light to the world. Then in his smithy he hammered out the stars, which she strewed across darkness with both her hands. For a time the light of the stars was enough, and the children of Dagdha grew and prospered beneath it, shaping the world to Dagdha's commands. A plentitude of great beauty was wrought in that time, and Dagdha hallowed it.

But Balor grew restive, though much that was made in those long years came from the labor of his hands. What he had built was beautiful to him, and he deemed the light of Morrighan's stars not enough to reveal all that he had done in its full glory.

And so Balor, who was called the Fomorian, went to his father and asked a great boon, that Dagdha should make greater lamps, one of silver, the other of gold, for those were the hues Balor loved best.

But Dagdha, being content with the labors of his children, and knowing the secrets of his own mind, which he had not revealed to any other, refused his mightiest son. And though Balor bowed his head and accepted this judgment, in his heart he was angry, and afterwards he began a great plot.

Working in secret, he gathered to himself other Powers of like mind, and sang great songs to them, and swayed them into madness. For he purposed to take the forge of Dagdha for his own, and in it build the lamps that were his heart's desire.

Though Balor was headstrong, and overly proud in his judgments, the ordering of his mind was stronger than any of his sibs, and he knew that he risked much. Therefore he determined to build himself a place of refuge, safe from the wrath of his father. For he knew that he would feel Dagdha's rage, should he succeed in all that he planned.

He went to the westernmost edge of Avallon, where the endless dark began, and built himself a great wall, which he called the Mountains of Guard. He carved these peaks of adamant, which could not be broken unless all the world was also broken, because they were built of the bones of the world. On a great shelf, or ledge, about the knees of these peaks, he lay the deep foundations of his guarded home, where he should be safe even from the wrath of Dagdha.

Into this work he sank much of his own power, and so hallowed it, and made it stronger than anything yet built by the labor of the Powers. Wreathed before it like a garland he made a plain that was wondrously sweet, full of running springs and silent lakes and great banks of blooming night-flowers beneath the stars. This he called Adamantillon, the Fields of Forevermore. And all this was a marvel, and his brothers and sisters were in awe of it, for they saw how great was Balor's power and majesty, second only to that of his father, the Dagdha himself.

Then, when he judged all was in readiness, Balor and his thralls crept beneath the stars to Dagdha's smithy, and being concealed by the enchantments of Balor, entered in. There Balor put forth his own power, and worked with the Living Fire from which Dagdha had built the world, and the stars, and all else. He made a great ball of silver, and another of gold, and filled them both with the Living Fire.

But before he could do more, he was discovered. Dagdha awoke from his slumber, and despite the enchantments Balor had raised all about, saw much that he had done. Then Dagdha summoned Morrighan, and together they came in might to the smithy, purposing to take Balor and chastise him. But Balor was also mighty, and escaped the trap, and fled to his strong place in the Mountains of Guard, bearing with him the sun and the moon, which he had wrought. Also, and of most importance, he bore away Dagdha's bowl, from which came a portion of the Living Fire, though only a portion, for Dagdha himself was the true source of that flame. But the bowl was a mighty thing, and its loss grievous. Balor took these behind the walls of the Horned Castle, and all his minions and servants besides, and defied the will of the Dagdha that he should come out to kneel in penance before the doom of his father.

The Dagdha was angry, and he directed Morrighan to take up her triple aspect, which was also Death and Destruction, and break the walls of the Four-Cornered Keep. But when she did so, though the heavens above and the earth below shook and trembled, when her fires were abated, those walls still stood unharmed, as strong as ever.

Then Dagdha knew all that Balor had done, and saw the snare that had been laid; for though with his own power he might destroy Balor's place utterly, he would also break the world he had built, and all else he had done in the First Dominion. This he was loath to do, for his own purposes were longer and deeper than Balor had guessed, and he knew that the Powers were only the first to enter the world, and others were to come after them. And in the beginning, the first of these late-comers would find home on Avallon itself, though later the whole world would be theirs, for their joy and the joy of Dagdha.

So fearing to destroy what he had made ready for this second coming, he withdrew; but about the Horned Castle he set a mighty guard, so that Balor could not further oppose what he had planned. Among the guardians he set to watch was a new race of things, dreadful and strong, which he hallowed with the gift of Living Fire, so that none, not even the Powers themselves, might fully resist the flames of their breath.

Of these, the mightiest was called Ar-Mogolloth, which in the speech of the Powers meant Great Worm of Fire, though so fierce was Ar-Mogolloth's scourging of the plain before the keep that many called him the Questing Beast, and feared him greatly.

In other lays are told the remainder of the tale, and how Balor was finally vanquished, and the sun and moon set as lights in the sky over both the Undying Lands and the world beyond, and of the great battles and greater sadness that ensued. And of this long holocaust only one of the guards survived the wrath of the mighty, and that was Ar-Mogolloth, who remained on the plains of Adamantillon until the world should end, as both a guardian and a warning of the wrath of Dagdha.

But these songs are sung in secrecy and regret by the Druids, who know and keep them, though not for common ears, and so most men know not of the First Dominion and the overthrows and tumults which brought it to an end.

—4—

"Do you hear that?" Conor said.

Fergus stopped, and turned, and lifted his head. "Hear what?"

"There, again," Conor replied. "High above. A flapping sound, but great." He paused, straining his ears, and squinting up at the stars.

For a long moment they saw nothing. Then Conor spied a flicker of movement far above, like a vast shadow slipping beneath the stars, revealing itself in the absence of light rather than its presence.

"There!" he shouted, and pointed upwards with the Gae Bolga.

But Fergus shook his head. "I see nothing."

Conor continued to cast his gaze upward, but what he had seen didn't show itself again, and the sound he had heard slipped away also. Yet he sensed a dark presence still, and stared about uneasily.

They had kept on without stopping since they had halted before, and Conor guessed they must have come many miles, though the red gleam of the Horned Keep seemed no closer. But by starlight the great plain was wreathed and hidden in shadow, and though the keep was plainly visible, nothing else was except the emptiness itself.

Fergus felt his unease, and said, "I don't think anything can sneak up on us, Conor. Even under starlight this plain is flat, and holds no hiding places. If it's coming, we'll see it first."

"Then keep a sharp lookout!" Conor said suddenly, because he still felt the strong hint of danger, though he judged it had now lessened a bit.

So they continued on, but went shoulder to shoulder, gripping their weapons tightly. Yet for all their watchfulness, the true shape of danger was hidden from them, for it floated high above on tireless wings, watching them in silence as they looked out for it.

—5—

Though Ar-Mogolloth was dreadful and strong, in the lost ages of his guardianship he had fought with those even more terrible than himself, and so learned stealth and wariness, for he had seen his own brothers and sisters immolated in the battles of the Powers, and come near to his own destruction many times. Therefore he flew without pouncing, seeking to learn what sort of prey had come onto his fields, and awakened him from the slumber of the Third Dominion, through which he had slept entirely.

His time had been of the First, and the first part of the Second Dominion, and his enemies had been the Powers themselves and their vassals, who were as strong as he. When those broils were finished, he had slept, though he had seen the coming of the Sidhe of the Second Dominion, but not their rise or their glory. Of the men of the Third Dominion he knew nothing, and so did not recognize the nature of the two who now crept across his scourged lands.

Yet he had been set here by the Father of All, and given a portion of his power, to watch and wait until the end of the world. His was the key to the passage across the marches of the castle, and laid upon him was the doom to guard it forever, lest another Power take it and hold it again against the Dagdha. For the Horned Castle was still the strongest redoubt in the Created Lands, whether Avallon or the world beyond, and Balor had employed it to fell effect before the time of his ruin. And Dagdha did not purpose that another should ever lay claim to its power, for within the Horned Keep still reposed a portion of the might of Balor himself, if one should come who was himself great enough to take it up and use it.

So Ar-Mogolloth rode upon the upper airs of

Avallon, far beyond the blasted wastes that Balor had in vain named the Fields of Forevermore, and waited to determine what he should do. Though his mind was quick, and his malice honed to a poignant sharpness, he had lain asleep a full age and then some, and was now only freshly wakened.

In hopes of solving his puzzle, he consulted all the songs he knew, in which he kept his own memories of the things that had vanished, whether he had taken a part in them or no. As he sang these to himself, his blood began to stir, for he remembered his own deeds as if they were done yesterday. And he recalled that he had been a terrible force between the Powers, and many had feared the destroying fire of his breath, even unto Balor himself.

This was the memory that stirred first in his mind, and then kindled in his belly, and the Living Fire with which Dagdha had hallowed him burst into new flame. But he still feared to stoop from the sky onto the interlopers below, for even against his intolerable flame some of the Powers had possessed wards, while wielding their own awful tools.

But after a time he decided that it was not Powers who walked below, for though the Powers might clothe themselves in the shapes of their desire, they could not entirely hood their true natures, which were of Living Fire, and so he could sense them if he put forth his mind.

Then he recalled those who came with the Second Dominion, the Children of Avallon, whom Dagdha also created, though lesser than the Powers themselves. But because Dagdha loved these, whom he had made with his own hand, he gave them the name of the Powers, Sidhe, which in the speech of the Powers was Fire, and so they were called the Manu-Sidhe, that is, the Children of the Little Fire. But in their own tongue the Manu-Sidhe called themselves Aielvanna, the High Elves. And though Ar-Morgolloth's knowledge of the Sidhe Aielvanna was less, he knew them somewhat, for he had seen them before his sleep.

In many ways, the two below resembled the Manu-Sidhe, being of the same general shape and stature, and not being great vessels of the Living Fire, as were the Powers. And though the Manu-Sidhe had been a dire race as well, especially when roused to anger, Ar-Mogolloth did not fear them as he did the Powers, for their strength was less.

So he swooped lower, though remaining in silence, and wrapping himself with the spell-shadows of night, so that the only sign of his passage would be a darkness against the stars, and nothing else.

Such was his stealth that he was able to pass over their heads invisible and unseen, though only the height of three men above the ground. But after the sleep of ages he had forgotten his own bulk, and the wind of his passage, even gliding upon his wings, was enough to alert them.

"There!" Conor shouted. "Again!"

This time even Fergus felt the approach of Ar-Mogolloth, which was like a thundercloud that bends low before a storm, though he saw nothing, and knew only that something vast was near.

Fergus whirled around, his bright sword glittering in the starlight, seeking something to hew. But he found nothing. Ar-Mogolloth had passed on by, and returned to the high air. But Conor stood still, and raised the Gae Bolga up, for he knew the danger was above them, and from the sky, not the land, would come their fate.

Both men waited, tense with fear, but when nothing more occurred, they relaxed again, though not much.

"Eriu spoke of the Questing Beast," Fergus said, "and as I've told you before, I don't like the sound of it. But I see nothing, though I feel it. It must be something of magic, perhaps cloaked and invisible. How will we fight such a thing?"

Now high above, Ar-Mogolloth listened to this, for his ears were as sharp as his eyes. But he didn't recognize the speech, though he well knew all the tongues of the ancient world. He decided this must be something new, that had come after even the Manu-Sidhe. Yet he was still uncertain, for his charge was to be a leaguer against the Powers or their vassals, and these seemed too weak even for the Manu-Sidhe, let alone the Uru-Sidhe who were Powers. He also remembered that some of his old enemies were treacherous and full of wiles, and he feared a trap, of which the two below might be only bait to draw him in. So he contented himself with the nurturing of the fires in his belly, and waited for a sign.

It was not long in coming.

—6—

Once again Conor remembered the words of Eriu, and bethought himself of her lamp, for surely this was also a time of darkness. It seemed to him that her light might reveal the thing that stalked them, as it had also picked out the path they had not been able to see with their own eyes beneath star-light.

"I have the lady's lamp," he said softly, "though you fear to light it in this place."

Fergus would not gainsay him now. "That was before, when I hoped to creep in like the thieves we are, secret and unmolested. But I know we are discovered, and we are blind. Yes, Conor, take it out! I would see what comes to kill me!"

Conor reached into his shirt and took out the flame that was there, and let it rest outwards on his chest, so that a star flamed over his heart. Its light was great, and fell upon the waste like a mighty fire, turning the blasted ashes to diamonds and silver.

But Ar-Mogolloth high above also saw the lamp in the instant of its unveiling, and knew it for what it was. For he saw a glint of the Fire Undying, and knew that its like was never given but from the hands of the Powers into the keeping of their own thralls. Such were the vassals he had been doomed to destroy.

He folded his wings about him and stooped like a hawk, and became an avalanche of green crystal scales falling out of the sky. Before him went the Living Fire, which he breathed out from his mouth, and with which he had destroyed utterly Adamantillon in times long past.

He bellowed as he came, and his cry broke the earth even before he put his full weight on it, for it was a shout of devastation, and an endless thunder of woe.

# Ten

## Ar-Mogolloth upon Adamantillon

—1—

To Conor and Fergus it seemed that the heavens had burst open and spilled down a great storm, and that what came upon them was like an ocean of fire and a trumpet of doom. All around them the dreary plains were cracked and broken, and they staggered as the land shook beneath their feet.

Then Ar-Mogolloth crashed down before them, as a rising wave falls onto the shore. His scales caught the green light of the stars and threw it back, so they were dazzled and could not see.

But even blinded, Fergus strode forward, swinging his sword, and struck the Beast many fearsome blows, raising a fountain of white sparks wherever his steel struck the emerald scales that guarded and girded the guardian.

Ar-Mogolloth was dismayed by the fierceness

of Fergus's attack, and reared back, his great eyes opening wide. And Fergus's vision returned, so he could see what he fought, and in his battle-wrath he laughed aloud, and came forward again.

"Back, Beast!" he cried, "or I will hew you to death!"

As he advanced again, he could see his own reflection as a shadow in the great golden eye before him, so he struck for that, and hit home with one true blow.

Ar-Mogolloth screamed, for now he was blinded in one eye, and his agony was terrible. Again he belched the Living Fire at his tormentor, but Fergus swirled the cloak that Myrddin had given him all about himself, even his head, and the fire passed around him, and did not burn him.

Ar-Mogolloth was greatly amazed, for though he did not know the nature of the warrior who came against him, it was now plain to him that these were girded with mighty talismans, such as only the Powers might give.

With a single coiling leap he withdrew a hundred paces across the burning sands, and sat back down, and said, "Hold!"

He spoke in the tongue of the Uru-Sidhe, thinking that perhaps this was what he faced, even though he could not sense the Holy Fire within them. Nor would Fergus have understood Ar-Mogolloth's command, except he was still within the light of Eriu's lamp, and by the power of that he was able to understand many things that would otherwise be hidden from him.

"Hold, what?" he cried, but he crouched with

his sword before him, ready to advance again. Behind him Conor stood silent, wrapped in his cloak, with the Gae Bolga hidden beneath it.

"I would know what manner of thing you are," Ar-Mogolloth said, "for you are new to me. Are you of the Uru-Sidhe, the Great Flames?"

Conor stepped past Fergus and faced the Worm, his own sword in his hand, though he kept his three-tined spear concealed. "I know not the Uru-Sidhe. What do you speak of?"

The dragon heard the ring of truth in Conor's words but was confused, for it was obvious to him these two bore talismans only the mighty could have given them—the star, and cloaks proof against his burning.

"Then perhaps you are of the Manu-Sidhe, the Children of Avallon that Dagdha made?"

"What are those?" Conor cried back.

Ar-Mogolloth searched his mind and remembered the other names. "They call themselves Aielvanna, the High Elves, for in their eyes gleams the Fire, though not in yours."

"No, we are not elves," Conor replied.

"Then what?"

"We are men," Conor said.

But Ar-Mogolloth shook his great horned head, for the word was unknown to him. "What are men, and whom do men serve?" he thundered back. "Are you minions of the Dagdha, or of the Foe?"

Conor said, "We serve the Land that Dagdha made! But who is the Foe?"

Now more than ever Ar-Mogolloth was certain

he faced some trick or stratagem, for in all the ages he knew since his creation, ever had there been war between Dagdha and Balor, and none were ignorant of it.

He still wished to take a better measure of what he faced, so he said, "Then where do you go now across ruined Adamantillon?"

Conor raised his head, and pointed with the tip of his sword. "To the castle, for that is where my doom lies! You are the Questing Beast, and between us looms a fate! But I must pass, and you must stand aside, unless you would share my distant doom."

Now, if there was one kind of thing Ar-Mogolloth did understand, it was the workings of dooms, for the ages of his life had hinged on many. But in the end all dooms died in fire, and he knew it. So he reared himself up and laughed, and flames dripped from his great fangs.

"Not hence, but here your doom lies, oh, man, and I bring it to you now! For my own doom is to never stand aside, as I am the living leaguer about the Horned Keep until the world shall end!"

Then he launched himself again into the air, and blasted his flames all about. But he had already seen how the cloaks they wore protected them from the fire, and his eye was wounded also. Therefore he purposed something else—for he was unlike lesser beasts in that he was armored and covered in crystal scales both top and bottom, and had no weakness in any place except his eyes. So he made to settle on them and crush them with his weight.

Fergus gave out a great battle cry and raised his sword, but Ar-Mogolloth didn't fear him, because he'd already seen his hide was proof against that blade. He came down toward Fergus first, because the other one had not struck at him, and he regarded Fergus as the more mighty and dangerous of the two.

But as he sought to crush Fergus, he didn't see Conor fling back his cloak and reveal the Gae Bolga as he ran beneath the beast. And so Ar-Mogolloth, the Worm of Fire, fell with all his weight onto the points of the one weapon that could pierce his armor, as it had been forged anew for that purpose, though Conor knew it not.

The Worm was punctured with a great wound, and the fire within him poured forth. But Conor covered himself with his cloak again, except for the hand that wielded the Gae Bolga. And so he was burned, and ever after the memory of fire ran in the veins of that arm. But he remained steady, and his spear tore ever wider rents in Ar-Mogolloth's body, until the great dragon could take no more, and heaved himself away.

Ar-Mogolloth crawled slowly backwards, his guts torn and hurt, and his fires stilled. For he saw that the doom of this man was indeed greater than his own power, and he must let him pass. And though wounded, the dragon was still strong and quick, so before Conor could say or do anything else, Ar-Mogolloth had retreated many paces, and was still withdrawing as he spoke a final time:

"Then pass, man, for though I know not what you are, I know who you are, and I will remember all you have done this day. Look for me again, should you come this way!"

Conor heard all this, and raised the Gae Bolga again, and saw that it glowed with an unearthly light, for it was drenched with the fire of dragon's blood. But Ar-Mogolloth was gone, scurrying back to his lair to lick his wounds and wait.

Conor stared at the Gae Bolga, and watched as its light slowly died, and it returned to mere gleaming silver beneath starlight, though perhaps brighter than it had been, in the glow of Eriu's lamp.

"I will name you Dragon's Bane," he said softly, "for you are mightier than I guessed."

Behind him, Fergus groaned. Conor lowered the Gae Bolga and turned toward him, for he feared Fergus had been wounded unto death.

—2—

"Fergus!" But he heard no answer, and Fergus was nowhere to be seen.

Conor rushed forward, looking all around, and finally saw by Eriu's light a crumpled figure sprawled not far away. He ran to him and knelt, and lifted up his head.

"Fergus . . . oh, Fergus!" Conor was dismayed, for the warrior's weight in his arms was still and dead, and Fergus's eyes were closed. Conor set him back down, and leaned forward, and put his head on Fergus's chest, but he heard no heartbeat. He could see or feel no movement there, because

Fergus did not seem to breathe. Then Conor knew that the dragon's fumes were baneful with more than fire, and Fergus had been stricken with his breath alone.

But as he stared at Fergus's slack features, he saw no sign of pain, only a strange kind of peace, as if his friend was only resting. That gave him an idea. He took the silver chain from his neck and raised it up, so that the light of the star fell all over Fergus. Holding his hands together as he knelt, he lifted his head and cried out his prayer.

"Oh, lady, if you would help me, then help me now, not for myself, but for him! If he still lives, guard my friend, and wrap him in the sleep of the Sidhe, so that no more hurt can come to him! And if such sleep can heal, for you called it blessed, then let it be so! This I pray to you, in memory of what we have done together!"

So he knelt beneath the stars, bearing up a star, and waited for a sign. After a while his hope began to fail, for it seemed that his prayer would not be answered. Then, far away, he heard a sound as of distant voices raised in joyful song, and it seemed to him that for a moment he was ringed with forces invisible to his eyes, but present and watchful nonetheless. He felt a stirring in his bones and a quickening in his veins, and then the burning pain of his own wound vanished away, and he felt whole again.

He looked down and saw Fergus lying unchanged, but when he touched him, his flesh was as cold and remote and hard as the stones on which he rested.

"Oh, thank you, lady," he whispered. The song swelled around him for a long instant, and the star in his hand flamed more brightly before it returned to its natural state.

Slowly the song died, but its memory remained, and Conor's heart was the lighter for it. Carefully he replaced her lamp beneath his shirt. Then he found Fergus's sword and put it close to his frozen hand, so if Fergus should awaken for some reason, he would find it near. At his other hand he put his pack, so that Fergus would not want for food or drink on the barren waste. Then he stood, and turned, and gasped.

The great glimmer of the Horned Keep was close, looming in the dark, its crimson light no longer distant. Ar-Mogolloth, wounded and uncertain, had withdrawn the shadow-spells with which he barred the path, and made it longer than it was. Now it lay open to Conor and his doom, which the Worm believed was mighty indeed, and so made it easy for him to pass away into it.

Yet Ar-Mogolloth waited, and worked his power on his own healing, so he should be ready if Conor came this way again. But all this was hidden from Conor, and so he took up his path again with a steady heart, for he had passed the first of his trials as Eriu had foretold.

—3—

Quickly Conor crossed the dead wastes, and grew close at last to the portals and precipices of the

Four-Cornered Castle. But as he approached his goal, his determination, which had been so strong, began to fail. For the thing before him, which had been built before the sun and the moon, was awesome and dreadful beyond mortal comprehension. Like the mountain on which it stood, it rose in precipice after sheer precipice, and above these were high battlements upon which seemed to rest the stars themselves.

Every wall and tower writhed with living flame, so that the castle glowed like a brand torn from the heavens and rooted deep into the eternal stone. Compared to this keep and principality, Castle Glass, which before Conor thought was the greatest work of building in the world, was but a privy or a rude hut.

As he drew nigh to the central portal, which stretched two thousand feet above his head, the character of the plain itself began to change. The stars grew weaker, for in the light of Balor's keep, which had been the heart of his power, even the flames of Morrighan's stars were dimmed, though a portion of their light still shone through.

But the sands that had covered all now vanished beneath a twisted bounty of strange shapes. Conor paused, because he'd never seen their like before, and went to the edge of the path to see what he could.

Dark gardens grew on every side, curling and tangled. When he bent to examine one bush that towered over him, he saw every detail still preserved of leaf and stem and flower, but blackened into ash. He could not know what he gazed upon, though he marveled anyway. But here, so close to the walls of fire, even Ar-Mogolloth's blasting breath could not entirely erase what Balor had wrought, so this much remained as a memory of the gardens of Evermore, blackened and burned, but still standing.

He touched one leaf and it crumbled into fine powder, and he heard a tiny crystalline sound, like a small bell ringing. A great sadness filled him then, for it seemed to him he was perilously close to things beyond mortal hope, and in danger of losing his soul. Even ruined, this hedge called out to him, and reminded him of things he knew not. Though in it were also the shapes of bones.

He wrenched himself away, and went on, and eventually came to the towering maw of the keep. A deep chasm lay before him, and when he looked into it, he could see no bottom, except that fires danced far below. But there was a bridge across, thick and solid, made of the same flame-locked stone as the castle itself.

He paused, and straightened his cloak, and took a breath. Then, holding the Gae Bolga in his hand, he stepped out onto that great trestle. As soon as he did, from all around, even the air itself, he heard a long, sad tone, more dreadful than even the cry of Ar-Mogolloth, and piercing far more deeply.

For if his and Fergus's mounting of Adamantillon had been a deed of heroes, here he entered the place most hallowed in all the worlds, except for the halls of the Dagdha himself; and of all those Children of the Third Dominion, he was but the second to put his boots on these living stones. Only one other had come here before him, but that one's feet had not felt the burning sands of Ilmarin's knee, for Ar-Mogolloth himself had borne that one across. But that is told in another tale, one of wrath and woe, and Conor knew nothing of it.

He passed beneath a lintel so high he could not see it for the fires all around, and so went from beneath the stars, and entered into the living tomb of the Sleeping King, and was changed forever.

Not the least of Conor's labors was the trek that followed, as he sought the place that was doomed. The Horned Keep seemed empty to him, though the dust that piled thickly on hall and stair was of rubies, and as he strode ever upward, he was covered with a thin powder of fire, and gleamed like a torch.

The light was all red, and cast ruddy shadows on his cheeks. Indeed, after the chill of the plain, it grew warmer as he climbed, until he sweated and his face was covered with shimmering crimson beads. But always he went up, for he sensed that his goal was high and not buried, and he who slept here would not hide beneath earth, but rather seek the loftiest tower of this place.

He climbed stairs higher and more steep than the cliffs that threw back the sea from the Land of his birth, and hiked down halls so long he stopped many times to rest and eat, and even to sleep. But nothing disturbed him, for the place was empty, and the only sound that of his own steps, echoing and forlorn.

At long last he came to a pair of great carven doors, the left-hand one of silver, and the right, of gold. As he stood before them, he again heard the tone that had first greeted him as he entered. Then in silence the doors slowly opened, and he saw before him the Hall of the Inner Watch, and the four who awaited him there.

—5—

They stood ten paces beyond the threshold, and when he saw them, Conor gave a cry and raised his triple spear, for they were fearsome.

Twice as tall as normal men they stood, and broader, like great walls, armored in steel and gold, and with silver helms. Their faces shone with a terrible light, the light of Avallon before the stars, the gleam of the Uru-Sidhe that had lit the world beforetimes.

Each bore a greatsword whose blade was longer than Conor's own body, and as he stared, they showed him those blades, both edge and point.

"Hold," Conor cried, and brandished his Gae Bolga at them. "I come on an errand of doom, and none may stay my passage."

But the tallest laughed out loud.

"Would you threaten me with that tooth-picker, boy? If you come to battle any of us, best you bring a true weapon, and not something fit for pitching hay." But even as he spoke, he lowered his sword, and stepped back. His fellows did likewise.

Conor lifted his Gae Bolga higher, and said, "This is Dragon's Bane, for with it I pierced the Questing Beast on the plains beyond these walls, and the Beast gave way and let me pass. So should you do!"

With that, the eyes of the four guardians grew wide with wonder, and they bowed to him, and bade him enter. Conor waited one watchful moment, but saw no deception, then walked across the threshold into the topless chamber beyond.

As soon as he entered, Conor stopped again, because the majesty of the great room dazed and dazzled him. From the groins and grottos of the high ceilings fell brazen lamps lit with more candles than there were people in all the Land that Conor knew of. The light of these seemed brighter even than the sun, and it reflected and threw back the crimson fire caught in the walls.

Thick carpets of a like Conor had never seen made his steps soft and silent as he crossed toward a vast, round table set in the center of the room. Ranged about the table were five chairs, or thrones, four of them larger than any mortal man might use, but the fifth was for a giant only. Snowy cloths covered the table, and it was laden with golden plates and dishes, and fine utensils of silver and steel, and crystal jugs and bowls, and much else that gleamed and glittered. But all these were empty, as if waiting for a meal to be served.

In all this grandeur Conor felt small and dirty, in his drab gray cloak, bearing his lumpy pack, and marked with the smoke and grit of his trials on Adamantillon. The four took their seats, and the mightiest of them looked at Conor and said, "Climb up on your chair, for it is the one that remains for you." There was the sound of hidden laughter in his voice, as if he told a joke that Conor couldn't understand.

Conor ignored the joke and climbed up, though he kept his sword and Gae Bolga close to hand. But when he was seated, the top of his head didn't even reach the table, and he heard them laugh again.

He put his pack beneath him, and raised himself until his face peeped over the edge of the table-top, like a mole peering from its hole across a white snowbank.

For a moment there was silence, as they stared at each other. Then Conor said, "My name is Conor. I am told you are the Four Watchmen, but your names aren't known to me. What may I call you?"

One said, "I am Fionn." And the second, "My name is Cumhal." "Call me Manannan," said the third. The fourth, and greatest, said, "And I am Lugh. Why do you come here, Conor Golden Hair? This place is forbidden to all but its ancient master, and he may come only on bent knee to beg forgiveness and pardon from the one greater than he, who waits forever."

Conor had no idea what this might be about, nor did he care. He thought of the Land bowed beneath sorrow and a curse, and Catlin, Tully, and Fergus, locked like stones in enchanted sleep. For a moment he felt weary and afraid, not seeing how he might make his way past this hall to find what he sought.

In the end, he supposed he would have to fight his way through these giants, to come to the end of his doom. But he wished for a time of rest, to gather his strength. And he didn't know the direction of his goal, but maybe they did.

So he said, "I come on an errand of doom, to seek the Sleeping King, who is called Bran, for I need something of his to take away with me."

Lugh the Mighty leaned back in his seat and roared with laughter. "You!" He glanced around at his colleagues, and they were smiling broadly too. He turned back to Conor. "You come seeking a thing of Bran's, is it? And what might that small thing be? What knickknack of Bran's do you desire? Perhaps a shaving of his least toenail? A single strand of his golden hair? Maybe if he rolls in his sleep, he might pass a little air. Would that do, stripling? One of Bran's farts?"

Now Conor blushed, because their mocking laughter rolled over him in waves. But he saw at least they didn't fear him, and he might turn their mockery to his own uses. Better they think him harmless, and let their tongues wag unawares, than see his danger, and slay him. Ar-Mogolloth too had thought him harmless.

"No, I don't need any of Bran's broken wind, for I have enough of my own." He grinned and glanced at the table. "And if you will have these shining plates filled, maybe I will show you a few. They are mighty weapons, I assure you, and you will flee from them!"

At this their mirth roared up to the rafters, and set the candle flames to shimmering, and the crystals on the brass lamps to tinkling gently. The four looked at each other, and slapped their knees, or pounded on the table with their fists, and nearly fell off their chairs.

Fionn said, "A fell doom indeed, that a warrior should come against us with the stench of his ass!" He turned to Conor. "Lugh said to bring a weapon mightier than your tooth-picker, and so you have! Now I do tremble in fear of you, Conor!"

So Conor grinned, and nodded, and laughed along with them, and when they had grown quieter, he lifted one of his butt cheeks and let forth a familiar sound.

"There!" he said. "Is that not fearsome?" He rapped on the edge of the golden plate before him. "And if you will fill this with rich meat and creamy cheese, and this crystal goblet with beer, I will show you windy passings even more terrible!"

But where he had expected them to laugh again at his joke, they did not, but fell silent. Finally Lugh said, "Though this is our table, it remains empty. We have not eaten in long ages, Conor, for such is forbidden to us while we stand and watch."

Conor was puzzled at this, but he felt the prick of an idea. "And do you not drink, either? No wine or cold beer passes your lips, or even clear water?"

Lugh shook his head. "We do not eat, or drink,

nor do we sleep, for our doom is that they are the same to us, so that we remain as we are, always alert, and never let down our guard even for an instant."

"But aren't you hungry?"

They all glanced at one other. Then Lugh sighed. "Conor, our hunger is the greatest in all the worlds, for we have not touched bread or meat or drink in long ages. But who will feed us? None come here but those few whom we slay, and surely none bring food enough to satisfy our hunger."

At that, an idea sprang full-blown into Conor's head, and he began to see how the hand of doom had played out over all he had done, even from the beginning. "But I come with food, more than you can eat in a time as long as you have gone without."

"What!" Lugh cried. "This must be a cruel jest, Conor, for we have seen you, and even your whole body would not be enough to feed the least of us, not even for a minute!"

But Conor smiled and stood on the seat of his chair. He lifted his bag to the tabletop. "It is no jest. I will feed you, if you will."

Then Lugh's shining face grew dark with anger, and he also stood, and towered over Conor even as Ar-Mogolloth had done. "You are cruel to mock us, Conor. You don't know your peril! For I say that if you continue your jape, your life itself is forfeit, and I will slay you myself!"

Conor faced him boldly and said, "A wager, then! My life and doom against your long hunger! If I cannot feed you until you are as full as you wish, then you may kill me! But otherwise you will give me Bran's direction, and let me pass. What say you?"

Fionn growled, "We may kill you yet, boy, for impertinence if nothing else."

But Lugh cocked his head, and the wrath went out of his face. "I see you are serious. And you go knowingly into danger. Very well, we will take your wager. We will eat either from your hand, or from your bones. This I swear, by him whom we do not name in this place."

"Done!" Conor cried, and opened his pack, and tipped out onto his plate a great plentitude of meat and cheese and dark, soft bread. And he took out the jug of beer and filled his crystal cup until it foamed over onto the snowy cloths.

"Eat to your full content," he said, "for I do not lie, and I do not mock, but instead take pity on you!"

The rich smells of this repast rose up and tickled their noses, and their eyes went soft, and they leaned forward, their tongues running over their lips. Then Conor stood on their table, and lifted his pack, and filled all their dishes and cups.

# ELEVEN

## THE SLEEPING KING

—1—

Conor had hardly finished filling up the Watchmen's plates and cups before they devoured everything, drained the beer, and demanded more. So he made the trek again, walking around and around the table, spilling out joints of cold beef, salted hams, thick rounds of cheese, and enough beer to float a Roman warship.

This went on until Conor lost count of the number of times he'd made his rounds, and his shoulders were aching from toting his pack from plate to plate. For the Watchmen's hunger was insatiable. They ignored their gleaming utensils and shoveled food into their maws with both hands, and washed it down with more lakes of beer. The only sounds in the room were of lips smacking and teeth grinding, and much belching and other passages of wind. At which Conor couldn't help grinning, though after a while he began to feel as he had in childhood, when one of his chores had been slopping the family hogs in their sties.

Eventually he lost track of time altogether, and everything became a blur of greasy plates and greasier fingers, and the smell of beer wafting over everything. But they kept on gorging themselves, and his pack kept renewing itself. He wondered if he'd somehow gotten himself trapped in yet another spell, perhaps even a curse of some kind, and would be doomed to do nothing more than trundle provender enough for their bellies forever.

At length, though, it seemed to him they were slowing a little. Their hands moved with less haste, their cups were drained in a more measured manner, and the sounds of ravenous mastication grew less pronounced.

Finally Cumhal, and then the others, leaned back in their chairs and fingered their glistening beards. As they did so, they revealed vast bellies straining against their opened armor, like huge wagons out before them. Fionn stared about blankly for some time, and his head began to tilt forward until his chin rested on his chest. Soft, moist snores bubbled on his heavy lips. Then Cumhal followed suit, and after him Manannan sank into noisy slumber. Only Lugh the Mighty remained awake, and even his eyelids were drooping like leaf-thick boughs after a heavy rain.

"Ah, Conor, you didn't lie. In truth, you brought a feast for us, and I can eat no more. Long ages have I hungered without relief, and listened to the empty sound of my belly stuck to my backbone for want of provender. But you have provided with both hands, and now I am full to bursting. I must rest now, as my brothers do, for I didn't lie to you either. For endless days we ate not, and watched. Now we have eaten, and can watch no longer. But fear not. We will awaken again, and partake of the bounty of your magic bag. The beer, especially . . ." he added, his voice trailing off into drowsiness.

"Wait!" Conor shouted, and walked across the tabletop to stand before Lugh's plate. "You forget our wager. If I have won, then do your part. Don't forget your own agreement!"

With great effort, Lugh forced his eyelids up, and stared blearily at Conor. "Eh? Why, yes. The agreement."

"Tell me the way to find the Sleeping King. You promised, Lugh. Don't seek to escape me in sleep."

Lugh let out a mighty belch, and grinned sleepily at him. "I laughed at your three-horned sticker, Conor, and told you to bring a greater weapon. And so you did, but you carried it on your back, not in your hand or scabbard. So you have won, and struck down four Watchers who are mightier than you guess. But so I also perceive the power of the doom that lies on you, and know that your passage beyond us was meant to be, and that we cannot stay you, no more than Mogolloth could."

"Tell me the way," Conor repeated, hoping the giant would not sink away before he answered.

"The way? 'Tis over there, behind the tall crimson curtain. It hides a wooden door, and the door bars the resting place of Bran, who has many names besides. If you seek the king who sleeps, seek beyond that door!"

With that, his head toppled onto his chest, and his own snores rose to join the resounding chorus all about.

—2—

Wearily Conor climbed down from the table, onto the giant's throne where he'd sat before. He paused there a moment, regarding the wreckage of the feast before him, and the snoring Watchers scattered all about. For a moment he wondered at the size of the one who would occupy the high seat on which he stood. It was at least twice as large as any of the others. Yet he judged the four gathered at their table to be of the highest, for the light of the Fire remained on their shining faces, even while they slept. What sort of being would so shrink them, that they would bow their heads to the one who had sat in this chair beforetimes?

He tied the neck of his pack shut, marveling that even after satisfying the ageless hunger of the Watchers, it seemed no lighter or less full than before. He pushed it over the edge of the seat. It fell and landed in silence on the thick carpets beneath. He glanced at the Watchers to make sure none had awakened, then dropped the Gae Bolga, which he thought might be the only weapon of power left to him here. Then he climbed down himself, shinnying down one chair leg as if it were the trunk of a tree.

Once down, he loaded up all his gear and cinched everthing tight. He turned toward the crimson drape, which fell like a stream from the misty heights of the ceilings and lay in puddles on the floor. But before he'd crossed halfway to it, he paused, and turned back to the table.

He went first to Cumhal's chair, reached up, and loosened his greatsword in its golden scabbard. When the huge warrior gave no evidence of waking, Conor carefully slid the weapon free, though it was very heavy and took all his strength to lift it down to the floor. He took it by its jeweled hilts and dragged it far beneath the table, where it would not be easily or quickly seen. Then he went to Fionn and Manannan and did the same, and finally Lugh. Thus he disarmed the Watchers and hid their weapons. He didn't know what he would face beyond the wooden door, but he might come this way again, and he didn't know how long the four would sleep. He judged that even the smallest advantage might be a help to him in the end, a strategy Fergus himself had taught him years before.

When he was done with this, he again turned toward the curtain, and pushed it aside. Behind it, as Lugh had said, he found a small door. Small, at least, by the standards of this place, though to him it looked of normal height. He paused, wondering what that meant. Was the Sleeping King not a giant, even greater than his Watchers? Or had the door been put there to admit only those of mortal stature. And if so, why?

But he came to no conclusion, and after a few moments of thought, he took a deep breath, squared his shoulders, and pushed against the wood.

Nothing happened. He might as well have tried to push through the fiery stone walls themselves. He pushed again, harder, but with the same result. Finally he threw his whole weight against the unyielding planks, but all that bought him was a sorely bruised shoulder.

"Treachery . . ." he muttered to himself. He turned and stared at the four still snoring in their chairs. They hadn't moved. Had Lugh known the wooden door was impassable? But he had promised in his wager to show Conor the way. So the way must be open, or Lugh was without honor, and somehow Conor didn't think that could be true.

Through the door, then. But how?

He ran his hands over it, and discovered what his eyes had not immediately seen. In the center of the door, about the height of his chest, were three thin, perpendicular slots, so narrow they were hard to make out against the grain of the wood. But he could feel them easily enough. What were they?

He put his cheek against the door and squinted his eyes, trying to look through the constricted openings. He saw nothing except darkness. Either only darkness was beyond, then, or they were not meant to be windows.

Three. Each a hand's width from the other, straight up and down. He dug out his belt knife and probed the lowest of them, again with no result. The blade went in easily, but stopped after a finger's length, unable to penetrate further.

When he tried to remove his knife, it would not come, feeling as if it had become stuck in the narrow crack. He pulled at it, then took the haft and tugged with all his might. The blade resisted for a moment, then popped loose so suddenly that Conor went sprawling on the floor, the Gae Bolga in his other hand flying away to land with a soft thud on the carpet.

He got to his feet, feeling a little ridiculous, and dusted himself off. But when he went to regain his spear, he paused, and stared at the three blades.

Three blades, flat and thin, about a hand's with apart from each other . . .

He took the Gae Bolga back to the door. When he measured the distance by feel, for the cracks were still nearly invisible, everything seemed to match.

He licked his lips. Squinting, he fitted the points into the slits. He pushed. The blades slid inward, far deeper than his belt knife had done, in fact so far that only their bottom curve stopped them at last.

For a moment he stood there, holding the Gae Bolga still. Then, with no warning, he felt the iron shaft first grow warm, then twist in his hand like a living serpent.

He gave a shout and jumped back. But now, where the spear had been, was a great iron ring set into the face of the door, and the Gae Bolga had vanished. The ring was dark and rusty, as the weapon had been when he first found it, but on the lower part of the circle, tiny and shining, was a three-bladed image of what it had been before.

"Very well, then, not a weapon, but a key," Conor murmured to himself. He took the ring in both hands and pulled. With a small, dusty groan, and a puff of tomblike air from beyond, the door swung open, leaving wide the way into the chamber of the Sleeping King, and the doom long hidden there.

—3—

Holding his breath, Conor crept on through, his gaze darting warily back and forth. When he had passed beyond the threshold he heard another creak, and turned in time to see the door slam shut behind him with a hollow, echoing boom. Immediately he threw himself against it, but once again the way was barred. And though he felt for them, no slits or cracks marred the surface of that gate on this side.

He gave off and turned, feeling very much like a rat trapped inside a cage, although the cage in which he now found himself was very grand. He stood in a vaulted chamber, walled and floored with the same silently blazing stones as before. The light poured forth from walls and floor in a hot red glare, so that even the air within seemed to shift and burn. But here were no shimmering lamps or fine tapestries, or flowing curtains. Only the naked, burning stone and, so far away it seemed hardly visible, a tall, square structure growing from the flags, on top of which gleamed a steady golden light.

But Conor passed over this at first, because his attention was caught by the vast chamber's single most noticeable feature: the window or opening that constituted most of the wall farthest away from him, which filled all the space between floor and roof, and corner to corner as well. Beyond it glimmered stars of a kind he had never seen before. He began the trek toward this wide panorama, his mouth slowly falling open before the wonder of it all.

He passed by the great stone on his left and paid it little attention, though he did note that the golden blaze atop it was so bright it was hard to look at, much like the sun itself. But even this strange enchanted bonfire couldn't hold him long, not against what he saw when he finally came up to the window and looked out upon the Fields of Forevermore, as they had been newly built, long and wondrous beneath the first stars strewn out from Morrighan's eternal hands.

And so by gift of the enchantment that bound together the very stones of the Horned Keep on which he stood, imbued by their maker with his own power, did Conor gaze on that which only one other mortal had ever beheld; Forevermore, the finest and fairest thing ever made by the Powers, in the time of their glory before the fall.

Even from this height, a full five thousand feet above the plain, Conor could see it clearly. There were bounteous forests, diaphanous in white and pale pink, and kissed with an inner light that hinted at the coming of the moon, or the first rising of the sun. But those had not yet been created when these gardens first bloomed, since Forevermore was then only a prophecy and an intimation of what was still to come.

He stood mesmerized, breathless and unmoving—for how long, he could never later recall. When he did finally shake away from that paralysis, it was with sadness and a great knowledge of loss. For he'd seen the fate of those fields, blasted and blackened, and was pierced with the sadness and regret only the great had known before. All the grief of mortal man was but a portion of that, for though men had lost much, they had never possessed in all their time anything half so great, to mourn it after it was gone.

There were tears on Conor's cheeks when he finally turned away, because his heart was broken by what he saw, and what he now knew of the long sorrow endured by the Powers.

So it was that his face glowed with its own lesser fire as he raised up his eyes and looked upon the bier of the Sleeping King, set high upon a small mountain of stone that shifted and flamed with the crimson Fire that was sealed within. He knew that Fire would never wither, for it was like the blood of mortal man encased within his flesh, that shows forth as proof of life itself.

Conor walked forward, and slowly mounted up those great treads, each higher than his waist, having been made to lift up the feet of the Powers, who were much greater in all things and ways than mortal men. He labored and scrambled and heaved. All the time his back sagged beneath the weight of sadness, for his own doom to come, and for the far mightier fate he had seen above the enchanted fields of Adamantillon, that were now truly Nevermore.

At the top of the platform was a broad, flat space unmarred by any decoration. In its exact center was a golden bier that was carved with silver flowers. From this poured the light of the sun and the moon, and though he had to shield his eyes, as he came closer he could finally make out, in the heart of that blaze, the silent, bound shape of him who was prisoned there, fated to sleep until the end of the worlds, unless summoned beforetimes to waken by the doom that kept him there.

Strangely, while everything else in the Four-Cornered Castle had been huge, of a stature for giants or gods, the height of this bier was only a little above the stones upon which it rested. When Conor at last came up to it, it rose only to his knees, and he had a full view of the great figure immobilized upon his golden bed.

Fully four times the span of a man was the Sleeping King. His skin was like softly beaten gold, but his armor was of silver, and all shone with light. Yet that gleam paled beside the flame that shone forth from his face, for that was the light of Living Fire, from which all other lights were but weak and fading.

His head was as big around as Conor's chest, his features fine and noble above a golden beard. Beneath a tangle of golden curls were two eyes larger than mortal fists, but made of naked sap-

phires, blue as the memory of winter lakes beneath
an empty sky. His lips were slightly parted in his
sleep, revealing teeth made of great pearls. His
head lay pillowed above a perfect diamond three
times the size of his skull, resting on the palms of
his upraised hands. At his right side lay a sword
twice as large as those worn by the four Watchmen
without, but this blade was made of faceted crystal,
and poured out its own fell light. And finally, its
point half-embedded in one mighty thigh, was one
that Conor recognized, for he had seen it before:
the Spear Longinus had so desired that it had been
named as his own. Now, looking at it, Conor knew
that name, Spear of Longinus, was but an impertinence, for it was far greater than the curse and lust
of a single doomed wizard.

Conor beheld the Sleeping King, arrayed all
about with the Sword of Nuadu, the Stone of Fal,
and the Spear of Lugh. But though he looked, and
looked again, he could not find the one thing he
did seek; for he saw no cauldron, not even a cup or
bowl. Beyond, the great room was empty but for
this bier, and though he went all over it again, he
found nothing.

So Myrddin had lied to him.

There was no cauldron, or if there was, it was
not here with the Sleeping King. What had the
Mage said?

*Seek it in the hands of Bran the Sleeping Lord!*

But now he stood at the foot of Bran's bed,
staring up a giant's length, and Bran stared sight-
lessly back at him, only his head supported above
the Stone of Fal in his two hands. The hands of

Bran held no cauldron, just his own head. And Conor thought to himself at last of Eriu, and what she had told him.

*It is the head of him who sleeps I must have to help you. Bring it to me, and I will show you the Cauldron . . .*

But as he gazed upon the sleeper, he wondered how he could do that. For he was faced with a choice: to do as she had foretold, and hew off that great head, or honor his own valor, which forbade such a murder, for the Sleeping Lord was helpless as a babe.

Conor felt his quest teeter on the bitter edge of his own mercy. On the one hand was all his hope, for Tully, Catlin, Fergus, and their Land. On the other was his own conviction: that even should he save them all, the end would be forever tainted by the curse of the murder he must commit.

He reached over his shoulder and felt the haft of the sword resting in its scabbard across his back. Slowly he drew it forth, and stared at the sharp edge. It had been the sword of his father, and had come to him through fire and treachery, yet it was unmarked by either blaze or betrayal. It was clean.

Could he now sully it with foul butchery, even to save what he loved the most? For though he came as a thief beneath the stars, he had not purposed murder. But here it was, murder most cruel, or the murder of his hope.

What to do?

He moved closer to the bier, the sword taking up the shimmering light that came from that altar, and throwing it back like long sunbeams, sharp and dreadful as the waning light of a winter's day. He laid the edge across the neck of the king, but the king didn't stir. Though it came suddenly to Conor that those great sapphire eyes were watching him.

"I must . . ." he whispered. "Or all is lost."

He raised the sword, up and up, over his head, holding it in both his hands as a woodsman raises his axe to smite a mighty limb.

But the blue eyes watched him.

Conor felt the muscles of his back creak with the tension in them, as his body fought itself, and his heart and mind and soul as well. He saw once again Catlin, smiling sweetly, and Tully, laughing as he always did. And Fergus, with the gruff grin of friendship on his face. And beyond all he saw the Land that he loved, which was fairer to him than any other thing.

All of it balanced on the moment, and on the edge of his blade, and on his doom.

But the blue eyes watched him.

His knuckles were white on the haft of his sword as he took a final sip of air. He stepped forward . . .

And gave a great shudder, and fell to his knees, and then threw himself across that mighty chest, his sword falling with a clang.

"I cannot," he wept. "Though all else fail and be lost, I cannot do this." In his misery he knew that he had faltered in his quest, and the doom that now awaited him was both judgment and punishment, for he had made his choice.

Thus did Conor the mortal lie across the face

of the Sleeping Lord and weep, for now all was lost, and his fate was upon him.

—4—

Then out of the fire all around a third tone sounded, which was the same as the first two he had heard, a cry of sadness and regret that rattled down the ages like the tolling of a great bell. He lifted his head, and a mighty voice spoke to him.

*"Fear not, blessed warrior, for out of despair you find triumph! Yet in my halls a great doom holds, that only the tears of a mortal shed in mercy may unlock my chains. Rise up, Conor, son of Derek, for by your weeping alone do you wake the Sleeping King at last!"*

Conor felt the mighty form beneath him, which was made of stone and metal imperishable, and harder than the loss of hope, now stir with warmth and life. He threw himself back, and ran to his sword, for the Sleeping Lord was awake, and now sitting himself up on his bed.

"Lord . . ." he breathed in wonder, for in his arising, Bran of Many Names was like a great storm coming to the shore, or the lifting of the sun above the horizon at the break of dawn. Yet his face shone with the light of the moon as well, and his countenance was fearsome, and full of a dreadful joy.

Now the king stood fully upright, and in his hand blazed the Sword of Nuadu, which was lit with the light of the First Fire. He towered over

Conor fully four times his height, and looked down on him as a man might regard a mouse.

For a moment, all was silence. Then Bran said, "Do not be afraid, Conor, for in the end you did choose, and choose rightly. As so I have wrought better than I knew. For honor lives in the hearts of mortal men, though it may fail elsewhere."

Bran raised up his sword and said, "Receive my salute, mortal hero, for you are greater than you know, and I honor you, as you do me. For in the end you honor yourself, and all that you touch will one day be hallowed."

But Conor didn't know what to make of this, except that now his task, though freed from the curse of murder, was much the harder. For while he might have slain this lord asleep, now the king was awake. He stood as tall as a god, and his face shone with fell light. And in his hand was Nuadu, beneath whose edge all things, even the Fire itself, must break and fail. For Nuadu was himself of the Living Flame, that nothing might withstand him.

Conor raised his sword. Bran looked down on him with sapphire gaze, and nodded. "Would you then, Conor, who is but a mortal, strive with your mortal strength against one of the Highest?"

Conor took a stronger grip on the haft of his weapon. He licked his lips, tasting salt, and said, "I would, lord. For I have no other choice, and my doom is before me."

Bran smiled, revealing his teeth of great white pearls. "Truly I have made well, with the labor of my hands and the light of moon and sun in the deeps of time. For if you are mortal, Conor, you are better than I hoped, and higher than I guessed. I see your quest and doom, and as you have honored me, so I will honor you. No greater fate could any warrior find than to swagger blades with me, and face the fire of Nuadu in my own hands."

"I will kill you if I can, lord," Conor warned.

"You cannot. But you may achieve your quest anyway," Bran said. And a great light was kindled in his eyes.

Conor felt the lust for battle filling him up, and in his own eyes gleamed the light of doom. He threw back his head and laughed, for now he was fey, and though he faced a god, he didn't care. He was free, and young, and in his strength, and he held a mighty blade.

"Then let us begin," he cried.

And so they did.

—5—

No other mortal eyes than Conor's own beheld the battle he fought that day, overlooking lost Forevermore, against the Sleeping King awakened.

Long they labored, as smiths hammering steel over iron within the fires of their own forges. Conor struck many great blows, and Nuadu, which sang his own song, the most dire ever known in all the worlds, scarred long gashes in the living stone itself.

And had there been a singer to mark that war, he might have made a wondrous lay, of the strength and skill of Conor, son of Derek, on that day. But there was no singer, and even had there been, the tale must have ended in sadness and regret.

For none of mortal men, nor even the Manu-Sidhe, who were greater, or the Uru-Sidhe, the Great Flames themselves, might in the end prevail against that blade in that hand. Only if the One should come against him could Bran of Many Names falter, but so also would the Two Worlds falter, and all within them.

Therefore all dooms fail in fire, and Nuadu was the greatest fire. At long length Conor found himself against the bier, bending backwards, his muscles unstrung and his bones no longer able to hold him up. His sword trembled in his hand, and Nuadu, singing his songs of destruction, was raised high above him, thirsting to drink Conor's life.

"You have fought me well," Bran said, holding back his stroke for a moment. "Better than many in long ages of war. No mortal could have done better, save for one, but there is no difference between you."

Conor wearily lifted up his sword again. "I am not dead yet."

"Yield to me, Conor, and I will set you back on your path, and so you will live."

"No, lord, I won't yield. If you will slay me, then that is my fate. But I will fight my fate until the end."

Bran nodded. "I expected no other from you. Your name will be remembered forever in my halls, Conor. But though your name lives, you will not. Receive now my blessing, and your doom!"

Bran stepped back, and took Nuadu in both his hands, and raised him up high above his head. So he paused for a moment, his mighty thighs thrust forward, his back arched, his face a sheet of living flame.

Conor flung aside his sword, and leaped forward, and grasped the shaft of Lugh, the Spear Eternal, and wrenched it from the never-healing wound in Bran's thigh.

Bran gave a mighty cry, and stooped down as a cloud of thunder and lightning, but before Nuadu could cleave Conor in half, Conor flung the Spear with the last of his failing strength.

# Twelve

## Rescues and Retreats

—1—

A man is much greater than a mouse. But when a man tries to put his foot upon the mouse he may fail, for the mouse has the one advantage of his size, and that is speed in fleeing.

So it was with Conor, as he dodged Nuadu's downfalling blow, after he had launched Lugh the Spear. And while the sword that breaks all in its path cleaved Bran's bier down the middle, its edge did not touch Conor.

Now, of the Four Talismans, two are weapons of war, and two are not. Nuadu was the greatest of the first two, for none could withstand him, and he destroyed all that he touched. But Lugh was also mighty, for his blade was made of the same fire as Nuadu, and though smaller, Lugh was no less sharp. But to Lugh was also given a great boon, that he should be guided by the spirit of Fire whenever he was launched, and should not waver or miss.

Thus while Nuadu, as was his gift, destroyed even the flame-stones and golden bed of Bran within the castle, Lugh flew directly at his target, which Conor had set before him with the last of his strength. He screeched a dreadful noise as he flew, but that was nothing to the sound that arose when he met Bran's neck and with the fire of his blade severed the Sleeping King's head from his shoulders. Then the chamber shook with Bran's fall, and his body smote what remained of his bier into utter ruin.

The sound of Bran's cry blasted Conor's ears, and flung him away from the great altar on which he stood. Only by chance did that wind keep from lifting him beyond the window into the air a mile above the plain beyond. But the wind belched outward, and the Fields of Forevermore shook and shivered as beneath a storm.

Finally the tumults of Bran's fall lessened and then ceased entirely. The silence rang in Conor's skull as loudly as the maelstrom that had preceded it. But after a while he slowly got his feet beneath him, and stood, and looked out the tall window.

Below him he saw Adamantillon Forevermore as he had first seen it, as a waste and desolation, the killing field of Ar-Mogolloth. He shivered as he saw this, for he realized that certain fates of which he knew nothing had been changed. But he didn't know what that meant for him.

Every inch of his body ached, both inside and

out, as he turned and limped back toward the rubble that had been Bran's bed. The Sleeping King slept again, sprawled atop the broken stones, with the fire of Nuadu still in his right hand. His body still burned with golden light, and his armor flashed silver, but no light blazed from his face, for his head lay ten paces beyond his body, like a great boulder flung away.

Conor skirted the headless ruin and came up to the head, which was half as big as he was. The light on that face was fading, the blue sapphire eyes going dark and empty. Of Lugh, the Spear that never misses, there was nothing to be seen.

Sighing, Conor bent over and tried to lift Bran's head, but it was too heavy. Then, thinking that he might drag it from this place, he took the pack from his back and opened it, and set it on the floor. Grunting with the effort, he rolled Bran's head like a great ball into the sack.

When that was done he was close to fainting with weariness, but he had no choice except to continue. His doom might have been fulfilled, but not the end of his quest, and four giants and a dragon barred his way back.

Yet he returned to Bran, and stood over him in mourning, and stared down at his headless body. For even in his fall, the Sleeping King remained grander than anything Conor had ever seen, and he wept once again for pity of all that had happened. There among the cracked stones he arranged Bran's hands across his chest, and lifted Nuadu against his side. He could do nothing about the Stone of Fal, except leave it glittering amongst the other rocks, and so he did. But Lugh had vanished, and when Conor gazed on Bran's thigh, he saw that Lugh's wound had closed, and the flesh there was whole again.

When he had finished with this, and done all he could to show his respect for his fallen foe, Conor went back one last time to the window, hoping for a final glimpse of the gardens as they had been beneath the stars, before the sun and moon. But all was bleak beyond, and even in his own thoughts the memory of those groves was fading and slipping away. Such was the sadness of men and gods, which Dagdha had foretold upon the plains of Adamantillon long ago.

Conor found his sword and put it back into its scabbard, which he cinched tight across his back. Then he went to his pack, purposing to drag it behind him. But when he took it up, it was no heavier than before, which was such a miracle he thought Bran's head had somehow vanished. Yet when he opened it up, he saw the gleam of sapphires, and the radiance of pearls. So he tied it again, and lifted it to his shoulders, and so bore away the greatest treasure of the Four-Cornered Castle, the Horned Keep of legend, home of the mighty.

—2—

Once Conor had begun, he didn't look back. He came to the small door, and found it standing open. Beyond lay the Hall of the Watchers, and he stepped through into it. When he went to pull the door shut behind him, the rusty ring had vanished. But on the carpet before him lay the Gae Bolga, shining as it had before.

He picked this up and used it as a staff, for he was very tired, and his load heavy. He gimped like an old man as he crossed the great room, going as quietly as he could—but not quietly enough.

Lugh awoke and saw him beyond the table. "Hold, mortal!" Lugh shouted, and the thunder of his voice stirred his fellows awake too.

"You may not leave. None may pass in either direction, and your doom is done with. You may not go!"

Conor ignored all this and hurried faster, hoping to run beyond the door before they could bestir themselves to full waking.

"Fionn, Cumhal, Manannan, rise and take your swords!" Lugh roared as he followed his own urgings. But when he reached for his scabbard he found nothing in it, and Conor kept running.

The Watchers fumbled in confusion, for each had been disarmed, and they couldn't at first find their weapons. Finally Lugh, peering all around, chanced to look beneath their table, and saw their weapons in a pile.

"Under the table, and quickly!" he shouted, and there was a great scramble. But before they could arise again, armed, Conor reached their door, which now stood open like the smaller door through which he'd already come.

He dashed out into the way beyond, the tumult of pursuit rushing up behind. He ran through the dust of rubies, raising great clouds, and reached the head of the stair. There he paused and looked back, hoping the Watchers were bound within their hall, but it was not so. Even as he looked he saw Lugh hasten through the doorway, followed closely by his three brothers. And now they had swords in their hands.

A great chase followed. Conor fled ever down, stumbling along twisting stairs and galloping through endless halls, with a storm always behind him. Somehow his strength never failed, and he reached the bottommost gate a few breaths ahead of them. He ran out through the portal, onto the bridge above the bottomless fire, and so passed beyond the confines of the Horned Keep at last. As he reached the first margins of the blackened garden beyond, his strength drained away, and he could go no further.

He stopped, and turned, and took out his sword, ready to make his last stand if the Watchers should pursue him across the bridge. He stood, waiting with blade in one hand and three-tined spear in the other, when Lugh issued forth onto the flags of the bridge, and an instant later Cumhal, Fionn, and Manannan.

Lugh came to a halt, and raised his right hand, which brought his brothers up short also. "You think we cannot pursue, but you are wrong," he said. "For we are not locked beneath the Horns, but put there by another, and its doom is not our own."

He grinned and lifted his sword. "You cannot escape us, Conor. But yield, and come back, and you will sit at our board, and we will eat together. What do you say?"

"I say I will not yield," Conor replied. "Not while I live."

Lugh shook his head sadly. "Then you will die, Conor. And either way, you will go no further." Brandishing his sword, which gleamed like fresh blood in the light of the castle walls, he put his foot upon the bridge.

Conor steadied himself, making ready for the first onslaught, though in his heart he knew he would fail. For he was greatly weary, and they were four, while he was only one. Nevertheless, he resolved to give a good account of himself before he died, though no one would ever speak his tale.

Then a whisper sounded in his ear. "*Show them my face.*"

"What?"

"*Show them the face of Bran. They have not seen it, since it was walled up behind the small door, through which the body on which it was mounted could not pass. Show them my face. For my power is the greatest of all but one, and they cannot withstand me.*"

Now, this seemed a great magic to Conor, that the head in his pack should live and speak to him, but he had already seen great magics. So even as Lugh and his brothers reached midpoint on the bridge, Conor threw down sword and Gae Bolga, and lifted the pack and opened it. Then the eyes of Bran shone forth, and the light of those sapphires fell all around the Watchers, and they stopped.

"What is this!" Lugh shouted, and shielded his face.

*"You know me, Lugh of the Bright Spear. And you also, Cumhal, Fionn, and Manannan. For though you were doomed to watch, how did you think to withstand me, should else but watching be demanded?"*

Lugh said nothing, but instead tried to press forward again, even as the jeweled winter light brightened all about him. But it was plain he strove against a greater power than his own, for struggle though he might, he was gradually forced back. Then Bran laughed, and from his open mouth belched red fire, which fell upon the bridge and broke it.

When the smokes had cleared, the head was silent again. The bridge had vanished into the deeps below, and Lugh and his fellows stood beyond the chasm, beneath the high portal, waving their swords. But their cries were futile; Conor knew they could not pass the ditch which encircled them.

Conor tied up the pack again, and lifted it. Then Lugh let out a great laugh and lowered his sword.

"Conor!" he called out. "I would have killed you, but I am glad you have escaped. For you fed us, and gave great entertainment, and brought us a mighty doom. Go well, then, and take with you the blessing of Lugh."

The great Watcher lifted his sword in salute and laughed again, and finally turned away.

So did Conor pass the league of the Four

Watchers, and leave behind the Horned Castle forever.

—3—

With the last of his strength, Conor followed the path toward the outer margins of the garden of black ashes, where the power of the castle waned at last, and the might of Ar-Mogolloth now held forth.

He paused, breathing hard, and stared up at the sky. There was nothing above but stars, a great wheeling pavement of them, and Conor could see no shadow flying beneath them. But he remembered what the Worm of Fire had said. He was sure that somewhere beyond, out upon the blasted waste, the dragon lay waiting for him. He was too tired to face that, so he stepped off the path and scraped out a depression in the sand for his bed.

He pulled his gray cloak about him, and pillowed his head on the pack. In one hand he held the Gae Bolga, and with the other grasped his sword. He could think of no other preparations to make, and finally closed his eyes. But sleep did not come immediately, for though he ached with weariness, many thoughts swirled in his skull.

He didn't doubt he would have to face the Worm again, if not soon, then later. And Fergus was out there somewhere, frozen in the sleep of the Sidhe. As well, Tully and Caitlin were in that slumber, and worst of all, he didn't have the

Cauldron. He had a head, but what that might mean, he had no idea.

All of this nagged at him, and he nagged at it, while the stars turned slowly and silently overhead. Finally his own sadness overtook him, of what he had seen and done, and what he now understood about the loss and long suffering of the mighty. Against that, even the troubles of his beloved Land seemed of little moment. With that final disheartening thought, he slept.

——4——

While Conor lay far below, tossing in troubled slumber, Ar-Mogolloth rode the high air, listening to the sound of his wings against the endless dark, and considering what he had seen.

He well knew where Conor was. Nothing beyond the walls of the Horned Keep escaped his gaze, and so he had watched the destruction of the bridge and the defeat of the guardians. He had heard the voice of Bran's head, seen the sapphire light from his eyes, and watched the fire belch from his mouth. Nor had it escaped his observations that Conor still carried the Gae Bolga, which had wounded him greatly, though he had by now healed himself.

But what should he do about all this? Moreover, what could he do? He well recognized that a great power lay hidden in Conor's bag. In fact, he knew the power of old, and though that power had cause to fear him, he feared it also, for in the end it was the stronger.

Yet the shape of the power was less than it had been before, and Ar-Mogolloth didn't know what that meant. In the end, his confusion and uncertainty on the matter got the better of him, and he bent his wings toward the distance, and left the Horned Castle far behind.

Near the outer reaches of the waste was something he did know: the location of the other warrior, whom his breath had felled. That one waited, cold as the sands on which he slept, and as hard. Ar-Mogolloth judged that the one with golden hair would make for this place, but it would take a while. Especially if Golden Hair had to walk through the spell-shadows Ar-Mogolloth now laid across the desolation.

He stooped like a vast bird, hooded and somber, and settled to the sands beyond where Fergus lay. There he folded himself up, and waited to see what would come.

—5—

Conor awoke feeling tired and beaten, but a little better than before. He sat up and stretched. The movement brought a soft groan to his lips. He licked his lips, looked around, and saw nothing. At least Ar-Mogolloth hadn't come upon him in the darkness, which he supposed was something. Yet he still felt the dragon's presence as a dark cloud pressing down on his spirit. The Worm was out there somewhere, waiting . . .

He yawned and undid the top of his pack.

Bran's head was still there, but all its light was gone, and it showed no signs of magical life. "Bring me the head," Eriu had said. But if he'd known what that deed entailed, he might never have begun it in the first place. Had Eriu known? He guessed she had. She had given him her own lamp, without which he would never have reached this point.

Thinking on this, he pushed aside the head, looking for a bite or two with which to break his fast. He'd forgotten how long it had been since he'd eaten. But when he dug deeper into the pack, all he could find were apples.

He pulled one out and stared at it. In the starry darkness it showed only the faintest gleam of red, but when he put it into his mouth, it was as fine and juicy as he remembered all the others.

He ate two more, and this eased his hunger somewhat, though now he had another worry. All through his journey the pack had fed him a variety of things—meat, and cheese, and beer. But now these were gone, and he had only apples. The pack was magical, and like Eriu's lamp, it had already aided him. He wondered if he'd somehow exhausted its bounty when he'd satisfied the appetites of the Four Watchers. But that didn't seem right, either.

Everything he'd done, or been given, or seen happen on his journey had turned out to have some purpose. The pack got him past the Watchers, and carried out the head for him. The cloaks had turned aside dragon-fire. The Gae Bolga had both defeated the dragon and opened the inner door of the Horned

Keep. Eriu's light had found his path in the first place, and saved Fergus from further harm.

Now he had a bag full of apples.

He considered for a long time, but couldn't think of any reason, and finally gave up. He knew he could not have foreseen the uses to which his other gifts had been put, and decided that if this change was somehow fated, he would learn why only when the time came for him to know.

He sighed, and retied his pack, and stood. It was a long walk. He began it under the stars, without much hope, but with a great deal of determination.

Things unlooked for had helped him already. Perhaps they would again.

—6—

Ar-Mogolloth saw Conor coming from a great distance, because his approach was heralded by the same light as before. This didn't surprise the dragon. He'd expected the golden hair to light that lamp, for without it, he would never penetrate the spell-shadows.

The Worm now guessed from where that light had come, and sensed that he was somehow ensnared in plots of which he knew nothing. But while this might have given him pause, he still had his own doom and fate. So even though the warrior bore the light of one Power in his hand, and the living head of another in his pack, Ar-Mogolloth felt a cold breath of satisfaction at how his guess had played out. The golden-haired one had indeed come back for his friend, and so had come back to Ar-Mogolloth himself. The dragon recalled his promise as he watched Conor approach. When Conor was close enough, the Beast leaped into the air with a great crack and snap of wings, and swooped out to meet his prey.

Conor, trudging below, heard the noise and looked up. Once again he saw a great shadow beneath the stars, stooping toward him.

He wrapped his cloak about him and raised the Gae Bolga. "Hold, dragon!" he cried. "I have wounded you with this before. You said you would remember me. But do you remember it as well?"

But Ar-Mogolloth, circling like a great hawk before pouncing, laughed at him. "Yes, warrior, I remember it well! And I remember your cloak too. So you are safe from my weight, and from my fires also. But beyond lies your friend, felled by the fume of my breath alone. I judge you may fall also as he did, and so I will put you to the test!"

"Perhaps I have greater help than those!" Conor cried back. And with that he set down his pack and opened it, hoping once again to see the deadly blue light from the eyes of Bran. But instead of the head of the Sleeping King, all he saw were apples. The head was gone.

Ar-Mogolloth also saw, and his mirth rattled like thunder. "Did you think I knew not of what you carried in your pack? But I knew that Power from the first days, and have fought with it before. It is mighty, but I lived to remember the tale, and would have fought it again if needs be.

"Yet I see it is gone. A lesson for you, who call yourself man. Place not your trust in the weavings of the great, for their ends are not yours, and they may ever betray you!"

With that he laughed again, and turned his great horned head toward Conor, and opened his jaws wide. From his gullet flowed not fire but his own foul breath, with which he had struck down Fergus before.

Conor, seeing the last weak reed of his plan glimmering away, raised his face toward the stars and made ready to die.

A great cloud and reek came down from the night and billowed all about him. He swirled his cloak tighter, even around his mouth and nose, but the deathly fog entered into him anyway, and he felt his strength ebbing away.

After a time he dropped to his knees, and the Gae Bolga wavered in his hand, and its points bent toward the earth.

Ar-Mogolloth saw all this, and felt a great joy, for his plan had worked as he'd hoped. He dropped closer, the better to lay his breath on his victim, for he knew it was only a short time before Golden Hair would lie helpless before him.

Conor lifted up his head and saw the great jaws approaching, and a vast gullet scorched red with the Living Fire. In a last moment of defiance and despair, he reached into his pack and pulled out an apple. Ar-Mogolloth drew ever nearer, so that his fanged mouth filled all the world.

"Die, then!" the dragon cried.

With his last shred of strength, Conor threw

the apple straight down that maw. The Worm snapped like a hungry hound.

Conor fell forward on his face as the darkness took him.

—7—

"Conor! Lad, wake up!"

Conor heard Fergus's voice as a thin shout, bleak and far away. He thought he must be dreaming, or perhaps dead, and now meeting his old friend in whatever place waited beyond the grave.

"Conor!"

"Am I dead, Fergus? Are you?" he whispered, striving to open his eyes. But his lids felt heavy as stones, and for a moment he lay blind.

"What? Am I dead? No, and you aren't either. Come on, boy, open your eyes."

He felt Fergus's callused palm on his forehead, and then his fingertips gently urging his eyelids up. The light of the stars flooded in on him.

"Oh, Fergus. What's happened? Where am I?"

Fergus's strong arm took him and lifted him up, until he was sitting, though the motion made him dizzy.

"What happened? I don't know. I passed out, but somehow you defeated that oversized flying snake that tried to burn us. Don't you remember? Here, come look."

Gently he helped Conor to find his feet, and supported him as he led him toward Ar-Mogolloth. To Conor it seemed that a reeking fog still shrouded a part of his vision, for he didn't see the Great Worm until the last moment. What he saw then was terrifying, as Ar-Mogolloth's vast, snapping jaws loomed out of darkness before him.

"Fergus!" Conor shouted, grappling for his sword, but Fergus only laughed, and clouted him on the back.

"You don't need your sword, Conor. Come and see!"

Conor stood in stupefied silence as Fergus strode forward with his own sword, leaped up, and delivered a mighty, ringing blow directly on the dragon's snout.

"Turned him to stone, lad. I don't know how. Magic, most likely, though I didn't see it." Fergus laughed. "And if it was magic, then I have to say that I approve. Perhaps I was wrong, and not all enchantments are evil."

Conor passed his palm across his eyes, and his vision cleared at last. There before him, his endless bulk trailing off into the darkness, Ar-Mogolloth lay, silent and unmoving. Conor shook his head in wonder. Then he joined Fergus where he stood, and placed one hand on the monstrous hide.

"Frozen," he murmured. "It's the sleep of the Sidhe."

"Aye, the fairy sleep. Just like Tully and Catlin. How did you do it, Conor?"

Conor looked at Ar-Mogolloth, and then at Fergus. For a moment he could say nothing. Then a grin began to tug at the corners of his mouth.

"How? It was easy, Fergus. I fed him an apple."

Then he began to laugh.

—8—

As they worked to gather their things together and make ready to set off again, Fergus kept staring in wonder at fallen Ar-Mogolloth, whose size was like a mountain shattered and spread across the plain.

"I can't understand how anything that big and that ugly could submit to only a single fruit, Conor. I tested its mettle before fainting away, and it was the strongest thing I've ever faced." He shook his head. "But I can't doubt the evidence of my own eyes. And I'm surely thankful for it. Now one less thing bars our path to that cursed castle."

He gestured toward the distant bloody gleam of the Horned Keep. For a moment Conor didn't understand. Then he realized that Fergus had slept through everything, and probably thought this was still their first encounter with the dragon.

"No, Fergus, not so." Then he explained all that had befallen the both of them, while Fergus listened in wonder.

"And you brought out the head of this . . . this Sleeping King? You really did it?"

Conor felt a pang. "Well, I did, or at least I thought so, but . . ."

He went over to his pack and lifted up the top, but with little hope. Before, there had been nothing but apples within. But when he opened the flaps, he saw a haunch of meat, nestled against a single sapphire eye.

Joy rushed through his chest. "But I did, Fergus. I did bring it out, and here it is. Come and look!"

But when all was said and done, and they were ready to depart Adamantillon, Fergus shook his head and said, "Now I suppose we visit your lady again, eh, Conor?"

"Yes," Conor agreed. "She will show us the Cauldron."

"I can't say I'm looking forward to it."

"Why not?"

"Because I wonder which one awaits us there. Your sweet lady? Or the hag?"

# Thirteen

## Returns and Rewards

### —1—

At the place where the waste ended and the Cracked Lands began, Conor paused after his first step down from the sand and turned to look back.

The Four-Cornered Castle was but a tiny red gleam beyond the stars, shrouded upon the knee of Ilmarin. And near at hand, nothing but desolation. Yet as he shaded his eyes, for one instant Conor saw again the glory of Adamantillon as it had been, new under new stars, in the morning of the worlds. And in that instant he strained toward it, unable to bear the sadness of its ruin. But he blinked, and it was gone. He sighed, and began to make his way down, and never came that way again.

—2—

Overhead, noon and night divided the sky equally, as Conor and Fergus crouched, watching the stedd within the valley.

"Well, the cow's still there, at least," Fergus muttered.

He seemed entirely recovered from his ills, and Conor also felt much better. Their journey back had been uneventful, except once, flapping against the night, they'd seen a small shape.

"A crow, I think," Fergus had said. "Not a dragon . . ."

Conor chinked at the crooked rocks with the butt of the Gae Bolga. "I don't see her," he said. "It looks empty down there."

"It looked empty before." Fergus grunted, and stood upright, stretching his arms wide and working the kinks out of his back. "If you're determined, lad, we might as well go down and get it over with. She's either there, or not. Or her ugly sister. But we won't find out sitting on our butts here."

Conor chewed his lip, trying to figure it, but finally realized he couldn't. "You're right," he said. "There's only one way to find out. I'll go first."

"A good idea. Maybe she'll remember you fondly, and not send her sister to answer the door."

Conor grinned at him. "I think I made a good case for myself," he said.

"Aye, you young sprats all say that. But what

you never learn is that a woman appreciates style over stamina. Style such as a more mature man, like myself, might possess."

"I'm sorry, Fergus," Conor said as he stepped past him. "I didn't quite catch that. What did you say? Wrinkles, was it?"

Fergus let out a bellow of laughter and aimed a boot at Conor's rear. But Conor dodged nimbly, and they came down into the stedd grinning and chuckling, though Fergus's hand stayed close to the hilt of his sword.

All was as it had been before: the placid cow eyeing them from the kraal, the thin curl of smoke rising straight up against the stiff breeze that blew from the mouth of the vale, and the bubbling music of the spring as it emptied into the dancing stream.

They mounted the path and stepped from stone to stone until they stood before the door.

"Eriu!" Conor called out. "We're back!"

When the door didn't open immediately, he clashed the tines of the Gae Bolga against the bell beside the path. A great clanging filled their ears, and as it did, the door swung wide.

For a fleeting moment Conor thought he saw something terrible there, raddled and ancient, watching them with a doomed gaze. But the vision was gone as quickly as it had come, and Eriu herself, looking as beautiful as before, smiled in welcome at them.

"Well met and returned, Conor! And you too, Fergus." Though Conor thought she sounded a bit doubtful about the second.

She stepped aside to admit them to her cottage, and though he had been there only once before, to Conor it felt as if he'd returned home after a long journey. It was all unchanged. In the stony hearth a fire snapped and hissed beneath a fat black pot, from which arose a savory mist of cooking smells. The rafters hung shrouded in shadows, though he thought he saw the quick wink of black eyes in the gloom.

The table was set and waiting, but the bed beyond, though heaped high with soft pillows, was not turned down. His weight caused the floorplanks to creak comfortably as he crossed over to the table; he settled himself with a grateful sigh.

"Ah, Eriu, it's wonderful to be back again."

Across from him, Fergus plunked himself down, and began to finger the cutlery, his eyes turned toward the hearth. She was there, bending over her stew, her shadow stretching up the wall, flickering to the jump of the fire.

"And you remember me this time?" she asked, an arch tone coloring her words.

"Of course I do," Conor replied, feeling his cheeks heat a bit as he glanced at the bed. She gave the pot a final stir.

"'Tis as ready as it's ever going to get, Conor. Bring me the Cauldron, and I will fill it up for you."

"What? The Cauldron?"

She nodded patiently. "Yes, it will make a fine bowl for this stew. Just bring it to me, and I will fill it."

"But lady, I don't have the Cauldron. When I

entered into the Horned Castle, it was not there. I will tell you the whole story, but"—he shook his head—"there was no Cauldron. And so I brought you the Sleeping King's head, as you asked. You said if I did, you would show me the Cauldron."

"Yes, yes, I remember!" Now she showed some impatience, and stamped her right foot once. The fire gave off a sharp pop, and spat up a shower of sparks. "Just reach into your pack, and bring out the bowl. I know it is there."

Conor began to feel as if he had stepped into another dream, or maybe had never stepped out of one. They seemed to speak at cross-purposes. He glanced at Fergus, who was eyeing him warily, as if the two of them had gone mad. But when he turned back to Eriu, he saw a flash of something different before the hearth. There she was again, the hag: bent and dire, crooked with anger, teeth filed to points and spread wide in a hungry snarl.

And behind this apparition the fire itself had changed, grown wilder and brighter, and he recognized its light; Ar-Mogolloth had spat it on Adamantillon, and the castle had burned with it, as had the face and eyes of Bran the Awakened.

The Living Flame.

His heart leaped into his throat. He raised one shielding hand, but even as he did so, the vision shifted and swam, and she became as she had been.

"Well?" she said. "I'm waiting. Are you going to bring the bowl or not?"

He stared at her, but she remained changeless, her expression both imperative and imperious. Not a woman it would be wise to deny.

"I will humor you, then," he said finally. He opened his bag, thinking to show her Bran's severed head. But it was gone, and he gasped when he saw what was in its place. There sat a round, deep bowl, around whose rim marched a ledge of pearls the same as those that had filled Bran's jaws. There were two handles, one on each side, made of fist-sized sapphires. The outer skin of the bowl was gold, but the inner surface shone with silver. And all of it glowed with a wondrous light, the same light he now saw flashing in answer from the hearth as he drew the bowl out of his pack.

"There," Eriu said. "I knew you had it. Why did you hesitate? Were you afraid of me?"

"Lady, I . . ." He stood, holding the bowl in both hands, and faced her. "I didn't know . . ."

"I told you I would show it to you. Now, bring it here."

Moving as one mesmerized, he did as she told him, and carried the bowl over to the fire. He felt the metal grow warm in his hands as he approached. It seemed to him that now three figures awaited him: Eriu, fair and remote as lost Ilmarin against the stars; the hag, a bent and hungry crone, full of claws and malice; and last, a great black hooded crow, flapping above the flames, dark eyes burning.

He heard a distant roar that rose like surf in his ears. The bowl began to vibrate in his grasp. Then from it sprang great gouts of fire that arched down to Eriu's hearth and kindled a thousand new blazes. All around him a fresh inferno boiled up, and he thought he would be consumed. But the fire only touched him with the softest warmth, and after a while it subsided.

Only Eriu stood there, ladling a rich, chunky gravy out of her pot and into his bowl.

"Take it back to Fergus, and the both of you eat, for this stew is blessed as none other. As you dine, think of exiled Balor, and poor Morrighan, who against all love and law, loved him."

Shaking with wonder, Conor returned to the table. There he and Fergus ate the finest meal of their lives, though Eriu would not join them in their feast, but sat aside, nibbling on a crust and watching them. When they were done, they wiped the bowl to shining cleanness with scraps of bread, and ate those too.

Conor patted his belly, and Fergus let out an answering belch. Then Conor said, "Tell me, lady, is this what I have sought? Is this truly the Cauldron of—"

But before he could say further, she raised one hand and sharply cut him off. "Speak not the name, lest you attract his attention. He sleeps now, for the first time in ages, and much that was hidden comes forth." She paused, as if considering whether to speak longer. Then she brightened. "But this concerns you not, Golden Hair. You have your bowl. Take it to your magician, and all will be well with you and yours. I, Eriu, promise it! You have my token as proof of it."

With that, she reached forward and touched the stone that lay hidden beneath his shirt. He felt a great surge of heat fill his heart.

Fergus seemed to understand what was happening. He snorted, and pushed back away from the table. "I guess that's my signal to go off to the barn, eh? Well, I guess I am tired . . ."

But Eriu removed her finger, and sat back as well. "Aye, Fergus, it's time for rest. For the both of you, I'm afraid. Go now, Conor, and sleep for a while. And fear not! Your bowl will be waiting for your return."

But Conor shook his head, lifted the Cauldron from the table, and placed it back into the pack. "I am tired, lady, and a good sleep in the fragrance of your barn sounds fine to me. But I have risked much for this bowl, and would not have it out of my hands. If you don't mind, I will take it with me, and keep it safe."

She stood, and flashed her eyes at him. "And if I do mind?"

Conor also stood. "Then we will have a disagreement. But it will not be the first disagreement I have had over this bowl, and I won't shrink from it, even if it be with you."

For a long instant they stared at each other, before she finally dropped her gaze from his face. "Go, then. You have your doom. Sleep well, and I will see you when you wake."

"Thank you, lady," Conor replied graciously. But he was careful to see the bag tied tightly, and made sure he carried it with him as he went through the door.

Once again, from the roof-beam, he heard the harsh, familiar cry: *Caw-rawrk!*

The hoodie crow.

—3—

This time Conor slept without dreams, and wakened with a light heart to the half-bright, half-black arc of the sky. Fergus also seemed cheerful, for they were returning home at last.

"And not too soon for me, Conor," he said as they finished packing everything and making ready. "Now go and say good-bye to your lass, and we will set off."

Conor nodded, and returned to the cottage. But this time she denied him entrance, and stood in the doorway to speak with him.

"Lady . . . I don't know how to thank you. You have done so much, and without it, I could not have—"

As before, she silenced him with her fingertip on his lips. "Hush now, Conor. None of this needs saying." She paused, searching his eyes. "And though it saddens me, I think you will forget me again."

"Lady, I will never forget you."

She only shook her head. "Farewell, Conor of the golden hair. Travel light and swift, and take my blessings with you."

He nodded, and began to turn away, but she put her hand on his shoulder and stopped him. "I have given you my token," she said. "Now give me yours, for I will not forget."

He felt her spell then, and leaned close, until his lips touched hers. But only for an instant. Then she stepped back.

"You will forget me, Conor, and I will fall

away from your thoughts. But your Land will know me forever, for one day it will bear my name! So I say, and so it will be. Farewell! Godspeed! Good-bye!"

She shut the door.

Conor stood for a moment, marveling, before he turned away and went back down the path. Fergus awaited him by the stream, with all their things. They loaded up, and turned their faces toward the east, and walked away from the eternal stars, the light of dawn rising golden about them.

The last sound Conor heard was Eriu's spring, leaping from the rocks with the music of a thousand bells.

—— 4 ——

After a long but uneventful journey, Fergus and Conor returned at last to the land of eternal daylight, where the sun shone down on meadows heaped with flowers, on orchards that gleamed gold and crimson beneath a sapphire sky, on forests cloaked with ancient shadows, dark and cool. They came at last to the river, and found Tully and Catlin unchanged and unchanging.

"What shall we do, Conor? Did your lady give you a spell, perhaps, to free them?"

Conor shook his head. "No, she didn't give me anything. It rests on Myrddin now, and his promise to us."

"I have little faith in that wizard, Conor."

"I know," Conor replied. "But I have fulfilled my half of the bargain, and brought him the Cauldron he desired. I must give him the chance to make good his part before we judge him faithless."

Fergus glared at the silent shapes of their friends, but said no more. They left them there, and went down to the river, and floated across with all their gear, their packs buoying them above the water.

Fergus climbed up first, and hoisted Conor out of the stream after. They sat for a while, letting the sun dry them, as they watched clouds of purple and crimson butterflies sweep back and forth above the meadows.

At last Conor opened his pack. There was nothing in it now but the Cauldron, and a few apples. He took out two, and passed one over.

"I think this is the last of the magic in this pack," he said. "Perhaps all such things must fail. But these were good."

Fergus nodded, and bit into his. Conor stared back across the river at Avallon, wondering what would come. He raised his own apple, and took a bite.

Then it seemed to him that everything grew very bright, but all stopped moving as well. He felt his limbs grow stiff, and when he tried to cry out, he could not move. For a moment he heard the sound of distant singing. Then a shadow of darkness came across his eyes, and he saw nothing more.

—5—

Conor awoke to a bright dawn, and the sound of bird cries in the leafy branches beyond his window. He sat up and pushed back his covers, feeling wonderfully refreshed.

But he didn't know where he was. He gazed about, puzzled. His room was fair enough, with stout wooden walls and a well-planked floor. The bed on which he sat was fine, a thick, straw-stuffed mattress suspended on a net of ropes between solid corner-posts, and a fluffy comforter covered him to his waist.

Across the room his clothes, looking freshly laundered, were draped across a sturdy oak chair. Everything looked homey and comfortable.

He got up, and dressed, and pushed aside the homespun curtain that covered the doorway. Out-side was a narrow hall, and he followed it to the head of a flight of stairs. There he paused, for the smell of frying ham and sizzling hen's eggs drifted up the stairwell. He realized he was ravenous, and leaped down the stairs two at a time.

At the bottom he came out into a wide kitchen. A long planked table dominated the center of the room, at which sat several people.

"Conor! Sleepyhead! About time you crawled out of your blankets. It's nearly noon!"

A wide grin split his face. "Tully! Catlin! Fergus! How long have I been sleeping?"

They laughed at him, and pointed at an empty plate. He joined them, though he felt the oddest sensation. Something here seemed wrong, but he had no idea what it might be.

Catlin went to the huge fireplace and pulled out an iron plate settled on the coals. She scooped him up ham, and cracked a couple of eggs into the fat. When that was done, she brought it to him, along with half a loaf of oat bread still warm from the oven.

The food was as tasty as it smelled, and Conor said little until his belly stretched like the skin of a drum. But finally the feeling of oddness overcame him.

"Um, where are we? Somehow I seem to have forgotten . . ."

Fergus raised his head and eyed him with a worried frown. "Are you daft, lad? We are in the wizard's house. As you well know, for it was you who led us here. Now, I confess I thought little of the idea, but perhaps I was wrong. From what I've seen, this Myrddin fellow seems not half-bad. In fact, I find him quite likable. And he does say he can remedy the curse that lies upon our Land."

Just as Fergus finished, another voice, rich and mellifluous, broke in. "And I find you likable as well, Fergus. Good morn to you, Conor. Did you rest well?"

Conor turned, and saw an old man garbed all in gray come into the room. His hood was thrown back, revealing snowy white hair, and eyes so blue they were hard to look at. Conor felt a strange sensation crawl up his spine, but after a second his uneasiness faded.

"Are you Myrddin?" he asked.

"Of course I am. Who else would I be?"

"And you can lift the curse?"

Myrddin nodded. "You came to the right place, Conor. In fact, if you will come with me now, I will give you the means to do it."

The wizard gestured to the back door, which stood open into a small garden where a riot of flowers blossomed. They followed him out. In the center of the garden was a low stone ring-wall guarding a sweet well. Myrddin led them to it, then motioned for them to seat themselves on the benches scattered around.

"Conor, you will have to help me."

Conor came to his side. As he did so, Myrddin produced from under his robes a beautiful golden bowl, lined with silver, set all about with pearls, and two handles made of glowing blue crystals.

Once again, Conor felt as if something very important was right on the tip of his tongue, or maybe at the end of his dreams. He reached out to touch the bowl, but somehow Myrddin was facing in a slightly different direction, the bowl out of reach.

"That's . . . beautiful," Conor said.

Myrddin smiled at him, a kindly expression creasing his face. "Yes, magic bowls often are, even the least of them, as this one is." He reached into his robe and brought out a fair-sized leather water bottle. "You hold this while I scoop some water from the well."

Conor waited while this was done. Then Myrddin came back, the golden bowl brimming over with clear, sparkling water. "Hold it steady, now," he said.

He tipped the bowl, and poured water in the bag until it was full. When he was done, he gave Conor a stopper with which to cap the bottle.

"Don't let it spill!" he warned. "It is the cure for your curse! Take it back to the Land. Go to the spring in Galen's hidden meadow, and mingle the two waters together. You will see. The curse will vanish as if it had never been, and all will be well. This I, Myrddin, swear to you."

Conor stared in awe at the bag, while the rest of them clapped their hands together. Myrddin waited until the clamor had died away, and said, "Now, I don't mean to rush you, but it's time for you to go. I have many things to occupy myself with at the moment, and little time for such small matters as yours."

"Oh, yes, of course, sir. You are too kind. I . . . I do thank you. Really."

"Oh, Conor, quit spluttering and let's take our leave," Fergus said. "Myrddin has already made our horses ready, and packed our gear away. The sooner we are off, the sooner we are home, and the curse broken."

Conor nodded, and stepped past the wizard, who turned to watch him go. "The path leads around the corner there, Conor. Your mounts are in front. Just follow the path. It leads down to the ocean, and your long way home."

One final time Conor felt unspoken words crowding at his throat, but he couldn't think of what they might be. And Myrddin's great blue eyes were glowing like cold sapphires. Almost frightening, really. But wizards were like that, he guessed.

He bobbed his head once, then turned and scurried away. The others waited next to the horses. Without thought, Conor grabbed for his Gae Bolga, which stood next to the door.

"Lad, what do you think you're doing with that? Are you going to plant fields on the way home?"

Conor stared at what he held. It was an ancient pitchfork, all rusted and bent. His cheeks colored. He threw it away, the sound of their laughter ringing in his ears.

They all mounted up, and rode slowly away from the solid, two-story thatch-roofed house where the wizard lived. Conor felt a twinge of disappointment. It was a very nice house, but for a wizard so powerful, he'd expected something grander.

As the wizard had said, they found themselves riding toward the sea, and finally passed a rocky verge to reach the hard-packed sand along the beach. Conor led them right to the edge, where a small surf bubbled and sighed, though he didn't know why he went there.

"Hold a moment," he said, and faced out toward the water, his gaze drawn to the west. A light breeze had begun to blow, bringing the scent of deep water and salt spray to his nose. He stared at the far distant horizon, which faded finally into a soft blue haze.

Somewhere beyond, it was rumored, lay Avallon, the island farthest west, home of the Aes-Sidhe. As he thought this, a single clear note chimed softly in his heart, and he almost began to weep. But the moment passed, and he was himself again.

Just before he turned away, a glint of color caught his eye. In one small, stony grot just beyond him, the outrushing ocean frothed and boiled, and finally drained away. Left behind was a single orb, red as blood, smooth as ice.

An apple.

"Now, how did that get there?" Conor wondered. But there was no answer. After a moment he shrugged, and turned, and rode away.